A Keeper nice story

HARLEQUIN® *Presents*

Welcome to the January 2009 collection of Harlequin Presents!

This month be sure to catch the second installment of Lynne Graham's trilogy VIRGIN BRIDES, ARROGANT HUSBANDS with her new book, *The Ruthless Magnate's Virgin Mistress.* Jessica goes from office cleaner to the billionaire boss's mistress in Sharon Kendrick's *Bought for the Sicilian Billionaire's Bed,* and sexual attraction simmers uncontrollably when Tara has to face the ruthless count in *Count Maxime's Virgin* by Susan Stephens. You'll be whisked off to the Mediterranean in Michelle Reid's *The Greek's Forced Bride,* and in Jennie Lucas's *Italian Prince, Wedlocked Wife,* innocent Lucy tries to resist the seductive ways of Prince Maximo. A ruthless tycoon will stop at nothing to bed his convenient wife in Anne McAllister's *Antonides' Forbidden Wife,* and friends become lovers when playboy Alex Richardson needs a bride in Kate Hardy's *Hotly Bedded, Conveniently Wedded.* Plus, in Trish Wylie's *Claimed by the Rogue Billionaire,* attraction reaches the boiling point between Gabe and Ash, but can either of them forget the past?

We'd love to hear what you think about Presents. E-mail us at Presents@hmb.co.uk or join in the discussions at www.iheartpresents.com and www.sensationalromance.blogspot.com, where you'll also find more information about books and authors!

GREEK TYCOONS

They're the men who have everything—
except brides...

Wealth, power, charm—
what else could a heart-stoppingly handsome
tycoon need? In the GREEK TYCOONS
miniseries you have already been introduced to
some gorgeous Greek multimillionaires who are
in need of wives.

Now it's the turn of popular Harlequin Presents
author Anne McAllister, with her sexy romance
Antonides' Forbidden Wife

This tycoon has met his match, and he's decided
he *has* to have her...*whatever* that takes!

Anne McAllister

ANTONIDES' FORBIDDEN WIFE

GREEK
TYCOONS

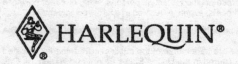

HARLEQUIN®

TORONTO • NEW YORK • LONDON
AMSTERDAM • PARIS • SYDNEY • HAMBURG
STOCKHOLM • ATHENS • TOKYO • MILAN • MADRID
PRAGUE • WARSAW • BUDAPEST • AUCKLAND

ISBN-13: 978-0-373-12792-4
ISBN-10: 0-373-12792-8

ANTONIDES' FORBIDDEN WIFE

First North American Publication 2009.

www.eHarlequin.com

Printed in U.S.A.

All about the author...
Anne McAllister

RITA® Award winner ANNE McALLISTER was born
in California. She spent formative summer vacations on
the beach near her home, on her grandparents' small
ranch in Colorado and visiting relatives in Montana.
Studying the cowboys, the surfers and the beach-
volleyball players, she spent long hours developing her
concept of "the perfect hero." (Have you noticed a lack
of hard-driving type A businessmen among them? Well,
she promises to do one soon, just for a change!)

One thing she did do, early on, was develop
a weakness for lean, dark-haired, handsome
lone-wolf-type guys. When she finally found one,
he was in the university library where she was
working. She knew a good man when she saw one.
They've now been sharing "happily ever afters"
for over thirty years. They have four grown children
and a steadily increasing number of grandchildren.
They also have three dogs, who keep her fit by taking
her on long walks every day.

Quite a few years ago they moved to the Midwest, but
they spend more and more time in Montana. And, as
Anne says, she lives there in her head most of the time
anyway. She wishes a small town like her very own
Elmer, Montana, existed. She'd move there in a minute.
But she loves visiting big cities as well, and New York
has always been her favorite.

Before she started writing romances, Anne taught
Spanish, capped deodorant bottles, copyedited
textbooks, got a master's degree in theology and
ghostwrote sermons. Strange and varied, perhaps,
but all grist for the writer's mill, she says.

For Janet.

CHAPTER ONE

"Mrs. Antonides is here to see you."

PJ Antonides's head jerked up at the sound of his assistant, Rosie's, voice coming from the open doorway. He leaned his elbows on his desk and pinched the bridge of his nose in an attempt to hold off the headache that had been threatening all afternoon.

It had been a hellish day. Murphy's Law had been written expressly for days like this. It was only two in the afternoon, but as far as he could see, anything that could go wrong, already had.

As the head of Antonides Marine since his brother Elias had, literally and figuratively, jumped ship two years ago, PJ was no stranger to bad days. He'd stepped into the job willingly enough, could never complain that he hadn't known what he was getting into. He had known. And oddly he relished it.

But there were days—like today—when memories of his carefree years of Hawaiian sand and surf were all too appealing.

Mostly the good days outweighed the bad. For every disaster there was usually a bright spot. When something fell apart, something else worked out. Not today.

The supplier of sail fabric for his own design of windsurfers had rung this morning to regret that they couldn't fulfill the order. A Japanese hardware firm who had been trying to track down a missing shipment reported cheerfully that it had never left Yokohama. And his father, Aeolus, had called to say he was flying in from Athens tonight and bringing house guests for the week.

"Ari and Sophia Cristopolous—and their daughter, Constantina. More beautiful than ever. Single. Smart. She's dying to meet you. We are expecting you out at the house for the weekend."

Subtle, Aeolus was not. And he never stopped trying even though he knew—PJ had told him often enough!—that there was no point.

A trickle of perspiration slid down the back of PJ's neck.

Not that he wasn't sweating anyway. The air-conditioning in the building hadn't been working when they'd arrived this morning. The repairmen had left for lunch two hours ago and no one had seen them since. Everyone was sweltering in the July heat and humidity. The latest temp girl had gone home sick because she couldn't stand the heat. An hour ago, PJ's computer had stopped typing the letter *A*. Half an hour ago it had flat-out died. He was back to calculating requisitions with a pencil and paper.

The last thing he needed right now was a visit from his mother.

"Tell her I'm busy," he said gruffly. "Wait. Tell her I'm busy but that I'll be there Friday for dinner."

Agreeing ahead of time to the inevitable dinner invitation—even though it meant meeting Ari and Sophia and their beautiful daughter—was a surefire way to prevent Helena Antonides from demanding to see him this afternoon.

"I don't believe she asked," Rosie said doubtfully.

"She will. My mother always asks." In his thirty-two years on the planet, PJ couldn't remember a weekend that Helena Antonides hadn't demanded the presence of all of her children within a hundred miles. It was why he'd headed for Hawaii right after high school and hadn't come back until two years ago.

"This isn't your mother."

He blinked at Rosie. "Not—?" He brightened and took a deep relieved breath. "Oh, well, if it's Tallie—"

PJ had no problem with seeing his sister-in-law whenever she chose to drop in. His older brother Elias's wife was still on the governing board of Antonides Marine and, as far as PJ was concerned, she was always welcome. She had good ideas, and she didn't meddle.

She didn't have time. While she had once been a hardworking full-time CEO, now she was a hardworking full-time mother. She and Elias had year-and-a-half-old twins: Nicholas and Garrett.

PJ brightened further at the idea that she might have brought his nephews to visit. They were a handful and a half, but he was always delighted to see them. But, he reflected, he didn't hear the sound of anything breaking in the outer office, so he supposed she must have come alone.

No matter. He was always glad to have a visit from Tallie.

But Rosie was shaking her head. "Did you forget? Tallie and Elias and the boys are in Santorini."

Oh, hell, yes. He'd forgotten.

Good grief! Surely it wasn't his grandmother! *Yiayia* was ninety-three, for heaven's sake.

She was hale and hearty, but she didn't travel to Brooklyn on a momentary whim. On the contrary, since her ninetieth birthday, she had expected the world to come to her.

"Don't tell me *Yiayia* is out there," PJ muttered. But stranger things had happened. And she had been on his case recently.

"You're old," she'd said, shaking a disapproving finger at him last month when he'd seen her at his parents' house on Long Island.

"I'm not old," PJ had protested. "You're the one who's old!"

Yiayia had sniffed. "I already had my children. I want babies around. You will need to give me great-grandchildren."

"You have great-grandchildren," PJ told her firmly. "Four of them." Besides Elias's twins, there was Cristina's Alex and Martha's Edward. And Martha had another one on the way.

Yiayia had sniffed. "They are good," she admitted. "But I want handsome babies like yourself, Petros, *mou*. It's time."

PJ knew what she meant, but resolutely he had shaken his head. "Forget it, *Yiayia*. Not going to happen." Or the chances were a million to one that it would. "Forget it," he said again.

But he could tell from her narrowed gaze and pursed lips that his grandmother hadn't forgotten what he'd told her last year. And he began to regret sharing his plan with her. Surely she hadn't decided to bring the battle to Brooklyn.

"Not your grandmother," Rosie confirmed.

"I don't know any other Mrs. Antonideses," PJ told her irritably.

"That's interesting," Rosie said, looking at him speculatively, her dark eyes wide as her gaze flicked from him back through the open door toward the outer office beyond. "This one says that she's your wife."

"Mrs....Antonides?"

For an instant Ally didn't react to the name, just sat staring blindly at the magazine in her hand and tried to think of what she was going to say.

"Mrs. Antonides?" The voice was firmer, louder and made her jump.

She jerked up straight in the chair as she realized the secretary was speaking to her. "Sorry. I was just—" *praying this would go well* "—woolgathering," she said, raising her brows hopefully.

The secretary was impassive. "Mr. Antonides will see you now." But Ally thought she detected a hint of challenge in the woman's voice.

Ally wet her lips. "Thank you." She set down the magazine she hadn't read a word of, gave the other woman her best hard-won cool professional smile and headed toward the open door.

Six feet of hard lean whipcord male stood behind a broad teak desk waiting for her. And not just male—a man.

The man she'd married, all grown up.

Ally took a surreptitious, careful, steadying breath. Then she swallowed, shut the door and pasted on her most cheerful smile. "Hello, PJ."

Even though he was looking straight at her, his name on her lips seemed to startle him. He took a single step toward her, then stopped abruptly, instead shoving his hands into the pockets of navy dress-suit trousers. He dipped his head in acknowl-edgment. "Al." The nickname he'd always called her by. His voice was gruff.

"Alice," she corrected firmly. "Or Ally, I guess, if you prefer."

He didn't respond, left the ball in her court.

Right. So be it. "Bet you're surprised to see me," she added with all the brightness she could muster.

One brow lifted. "Well, let's just say, you didn't make the short list of any Mrs. Antonideses I might have been expect-ing." His tone was cool, edged with irony.

And while a part of Ally wanted to throw her arms around him, she knew better. And any hope she'd entertained that they might be able to go back to being pals was well on its way to a quick and permanent death.

"I shouldn't have done that," she apologized quickly. "Shouldn't have used your name, I mean. I don't ordinarily use your name."

"I didn't imagine you did." The edge again.

She let out a nervous breath. "I just…well, I didn't know how busy you were. President. CEO." She glanced back toward the main door where she'd seen a plaque with his name and title on it. "I thought you might not see me otherwise."

His brows lifted. "I'm not the pope. You don't need to request an audience."

"Well, I didn't know, did I?" she said with asperity, dislik-ing being put on the defensive. "This—" she waved her hand around his elegant office with its solid teak furnishings and vast view across the East River toward Manhattan's famous skyline "—is not exactly the 'you' I remember."

It might not have been the Vatican, but it wasn't a tiny studio apartment above Mrs. Chang's garage, either.

PJ shrugged. "It's been years, Al. Things change. You've changed. Grown up. Made a name for yourself, haven't you?"

There was challenge in his words, and they set Ally's teeth on edge, but she had to acknowledge the truth of them. "Yes."

And she made herself stand still under the long, assessing gaze that took a leisurely lingering stroll up from her toes to her head, even as it made her tingle with unwanted awareness.

"Very nice." A corner of his mouth quirked in a cool deliberate smile. "I've changed, too," he added, as if she needed it pointed out.

"You own a tie."

"Two of them."

"And a suit."

"For my sins."

"You've done well."

"I always did well, Al," he said easily, coming around the desk now, letting her feel the force of his presence at even closer hand, "even when I was a beach bum."

It was hard to imagine this man as a "beach bum," but she knew what he meant. When she had known Peter Antonides, he had never been about the fast track, never cared about wealth and ambition. He'd only cared about living life the way he wanted—a life on the beach, doing what interested him.

"Yes," she nodded. "I thought…I mean, I'm surprised you left it. It was what you liked. What you wanted."

But PJ shook his head and shoved a lock of hair off his forehead as he propped a hip against the corner of his desk. "What I wanted was the freedom to be me. To get away from everyone else's expectations but my own. I did on the beach. And I'm still free now. This is my choice. No one pushed me. I'm here because I want to be. And it doesn't define me." He paused, then fixed his gaze intently on her. "But I'm not the point. What about you? No, wait." He shoved away from the desk. "Sit down." He nodded to the armchairs by the window overlooking the East River. "I'll get Rosie to bring us some coffee. Or would you rather have iced tea?"

She hadn't come to sit down and be social. "I don't need anything," she said quickly. "I can't stay."

"After ten years? Well, five since I last saw you. But don't tell me you just 'dropped in'?" He arched a skeptical brow. "No, you didn't, Al. You came specifically to see me. You said so. Sit down." It wasn't an invitation this time. It was an order. He punched the intercom. "Rosie. Can we have some iced tea, please? Thanks."

Ally took a deep breath. He even sounded like a CEO. Brisk, no nonsense. In command. Of course he had always had those qualities, Ally realized. But he'd never been in charge of anyone but himself when she'd known him.

Reluctantly she sat. He was right, of course, she had come to see him. But she'd expected the visit to be perfunctory. And the fact that he was making it into something else—something social, something extended even by a few minutes—was undermining her plans.

It wasn't personal, she assured herself. At least not very. And PJ didn't care. She was sure about that. This was simply a hurdle to be jumped. One she should have jumped a long time ago.

She needed to do this, make her peace with PJ, put the past behind her. Move on.

And if doing so meant sitting down and conversing with him for a few minutes first, fine. She could do that.

It would be good for her, actually. It would prove to her that she was doing the right thing.

So she sat down, perched on the edge of one of the armchairs overlooking the East River and downtown Manhattan and tried to muster the easy casual charm she was known for.

But it was hard to be casual and polite and basically indifferent when all she really wanted to do was just feast her eyes on him.

PJ Antonides had always been drop-dead handsome in a rugged, windblown, seaswept sort of way. Not a man she'd ever imagined in a suit.

He hadn't even worn one to their wedding. Not that it had been a formal occasion. It had been five minutes in a courthouse office, paid fees, repeated vows, scrawled signatures, after which they'd come blinking out into the sunlight—married.

Now she looked at him and tried to find the carefree young man he'd been inside this older, harder, sharper version.

His lean face wasn't as tanned as she remembered, and the lines around his eyes were deeper. But those eyes were still the deep intense green of the jade dragon that had been her grandmother's favorite piece. His formerly tangled dark hair was now cut reasonably short and definitely neat with very little length to tangle, though it was ruffled a bit, as if he'd recently run his fingers through it. His shoulders were broader. And though jacketless at the moment, apparently PJ really did own a suit. She could see its navy jacket tossed over the back of his chair.

He obviously owned a dress shirt, too—a narrow-striped, pale-gray-and-white one. He had its long sleeves shoved halfway up his forearms, as if, even in running a corporation, he was still willing to get down and dirty with whatever had to be done. Beneath his unbuttoned collar dangled a loosened subdued burgundy-and-gray-patterned silk tie.

Ally wondered idly if his other tie was equally conservative.

It wouldn't matter. At twenty-two PJ Antonides had been a sexy son of a gun in board shorts with a towel slung around his neck, but at thirty-two in tropical-weight wool, an open-necked dress shirt and a half-mast tie, he was devastating.

And he made her want things she knew were not for her.

She shut her eyes against the sight.

When she opened them again it was to watch as PJ dropped easily into the chair opposite her and sat regarding her steadily from beneath hooded lids. "So, wife, where have you been?"

Wife? Well, she was his wife, of course, but she didn't expect him to simply toss it into the conversation.

Her spine stiffened. "All over the place," she said quickly before any tempting thoughts could lead her into disaster. "You must know that."

He cocked his head. "Fill me in."

She ground her teeth. "Fine. Prepare yourself to be bored. As you know, I started out in California."

"You mean after you walked out?"

"You make it sound like I dumped you! I didn't, and you know it! It was your idea...getting married. And you knew the reason! You offered—"

"—to marry you. Yeah, I know." He shifted in the chair, then recited, "So you could get your grandmother's legacy, foil your evil father and live your own life. I remember, Al."

She pressed her lips together. "It wasn't exactly like that."

"It was exactly like that."

"He wasn't evil. Isn't evil," she corrected herself.

PJ shrugged. "Not what you were saying then."

"I didn't think he was evil then! I just...I just didn't want him controlling my life! I told you what he was like. All 'traditional Japanese father.' He who must be obeyed. He thought he knew best—what I should take at university, what I should do with my life, who I should marry!"

"And you didn't." PJ shrugged. "So, what are you saying, that you were wrong?"

"No. Of course not. I was right. You know that. You saw me when—" But she didn't want to go there particularly. So she started again. "I just...I understand him better now. I'm older. Wiser. And I'm back in Hawaii. I've been seeing him again."

PJ raised his eyebrows, but said nothing.

So Ally explained. "He had a heart attack a couple of months ago. I've always kept in touch with my mother's cousin Grace. She knew. She rang me in Seattle, told me he was ill. It was serious. He could have died. And I knew I couldn't leave things the way they were. I wanted to make peace. So I went back to Honolulu. It was the first time I'd seen him since...since..."

"Since he said you were no daughter of his?" PJ's tone was harsh.

And Ally remembered how incensed he'd been when she'd told him what her father had said.

Now she had some perspective, understood her father better. But at the time she'd turned her back and walked away. *Run* away. And even now she tried not to think about the rift between them that had lasted so many years.

"Yes." Because her father *had* said that. Her fingers twisted in her lap. "When I went back, I…I thought he might still act that way. Might just turn away from me. But he didn't." She lifted her head and smiled at the recollection. "He was glad to see me. He reached out to me. Held my hand. Asked…asked me to stay." She blinked back the tears that always threatened when she reflected again on how close she'd come to losing her father without ever having made her peace with him. "And I have."

"Stayed? With him?" PJ was scowling.

"Not at his house. I think he would like that, but no—" Ally shook her head "—it wouldn't be a good idea. I'm an adult. I'm not a child anymore. I have my own apartment in downtown Honolulu. I've been back there since May. I did…go back to the beach and…look for you."

His mouth twisted. "To see if I was still waiting for the perfect wave?"

"I didn't know you'd left Hawaii altogether."

"I can't imagine you cared."

Her jaw tightened, but she didn't rise to the bait. "I went to your place, too."

His brows rose a bit at that, but then he shrugged. "Did you?" His tone was indifferent. Clearly he didn't care if she had or not. "There's a high-rise there now."

"Yes, I saw. And Mrs. Chang…?" She'd wondered about his elderly landlady.

"…went to live with her daughter before I left the island."

"Which was a couple of years ago?"

He raised a curious brow. "I left Honolulu earlier than that. Oahu isn't the only place with surf, you know." He paused, and she thought he might explain where he'd been. But he only shrugged, then added, "I came back here two years ago if that's what you mean. You've been doing your homework."

"I saw an article in the *Star* about some former local turned billionaire—"

PJ snorted and rolled his eyes. "Blah, blah, blah. Newspaper writers like that sort of thing. Gives them a reason for living."

"Everyone has to have a purpose."

"Some people have better purposes than others." He shifted in his chair. "We were launching a new windsurfer in a new venue on the island and—" he shrugged negligently "—my sister-in-law said we should promote it. Suggested I give them a local angle."

The PJ she had known wouldn't have done anything anyone else suggested. Apparently her surprise was evident.

"It was my choice," he said sharply. "And look at its unforeseen consequence. I not only may have sold a few windsurfers, but my wife turns up on my doorstep."

Back to the "wife" bit again. "Er, yes. Something we need to talk about."

But before she could take advantage of the opening, there was a quick tap on the door and his assistant came in carrying a tray with glasses of iced tea and a plate of delectable-looking cookies.

She was completely professional and efficient, but her eyes kept darting between PJ and Ally as if she were in a minefield and either one of them might explode at any moment.

PJ didn't seem to notice. "Thanks, Rosie." He paused, then said, "I don't believe you've met my wife. Not officially. Ally, this is Rosie. Rosie, this is Alice."

Rosie's eyes grew round as dinner plates. "You mean, she really is? You haven't been joking? I mean…"

Rosie didn't look like a woman who would be at a loss for words, but she seemed to be now. And Ally was at a bit of a loss, too, at the notion that Rosie's surprise didn't simply stem from her saying she was PJ's wife.

He'd told his secretary he was married? Ally was sure she had misunderstood.

But then Rosie mustered a polite, slightly amazed smile and held out her hand. "I'm glad to meet you," she said. "At last."

Ally blinked. At last? So PJ had spoken of her? She turned confused eyes his way.

"Rosie runs the show here," PJ said, not addressing her confusion at all. He smiled easily at his assistant. "Hold all my calls, please. And get Ryne Murray to reschedule."

"He's already on his way."

Ally began to get up. "You're busy," she said quickly. "I don't want to disturb you. I can just leave—"

"Not a problem," PJ went on, still talking to Rosie as if Ally weren't objecting at all. "When he gets here, tell him we'll need to get together another time. My wife and I have things to discuss."

"We don't, really," Ally protested.

"And then set up a time early next week."

"Are you listening to me? I don't want to upset your schedule. I don't want to upset your life. The opposite in fact! I should have called first. I don't want—" She started toward the door, but PJ caught her arm.

"It's all right," he said firmly. Then he smiled at Rosie. "That will be all, thanks." And he waited until she'd shut the door behind her before he let go of Ally's arm and settled back into his chair again. "Sit down," he said. "And tell all."

But she shook her head. "What did you do that for? Why do you keep saying that?"

"Do what? Say what?" He handed her a glass of iced tea, then nodded toward the cookies. "My sister-in-law bakes them. They're fantastic. Try one."

"I'm not here for a tea party, PJ! Why did you introduce me as your wife? Why do you keep saying I'm your wife?"

He took a bite of one of the cookies and swallowed before he answered. "You're the one who told her that. I just confirmed it."

"But *why?* And she already knew that you were married!" It was the last thing she'd expected. She'd imagined he'd be keeping it quiet. Instead every other word out of his mouth seemed to be the *W* word.

"Yes. You're my wife, so I'm married," he said simply, and punctuated the reality by taking another bite out of a cookie.

"Yes, but—"

He wiped powdered sugar off his mouth. "You'd rather I'd call you a liar?"

"No. Of course not." Ally sighed and shook her head. "I didn't imagine you shouted it from the rooftops. You didn't say anything in the article about being married," she reminded him. "On the contrary, the article said you were dating hordes of eligible women." She could have quoted word for word exactly what it had said, but she didn't.

"Hordes." PJ gave a bark of laughter. "Not quite. I escort women to business functions. Acquaintances. Friends. It's expected."

"But they don't know you're married."

"Hell, Al, most of the time, I barely even know I'm married!"

His exasperation relieved her and swamped her with guilt at the same time. "I know,' she said, clutching the glass tightly in both hands. "I'm sorry. It was selfish of me, marrying you. We never should have. I—" she corrected herself "—never should have let you do it."

"You didn't 'let' me," PJ retorted. "I offered. You just said yes. Anyway—" he shrugged it off "—it was no big deal."

"It was to me."

Marrying PJ had given her access to her grandmother's legacy. It had allowed her the freedom to make her own choices instead of doing what her father prescribed. It had been the making of her. She owed PJ for her life as she knew it.

"Well, good," he said gruffly. "So tell me all about it. We didn't have much of a chance to talk…last time."

Last time. Five years ago when she'd come back to Honolulu for an art opening, when he'd showed up with a gorgeous woman on his arm. Ally gave herself a little shake, determined not to think about that. "It was a busy time," she said dismissively.

"So it was. You're a household word now, I gather."

"I've done all right." She'd worked very hard, and she was proud of what she'd accomplished. But she didn't want him to think she was bragging.

"Better than, I'd say." PJ leaned back in his chair and ticked off her accomplishments. "World renowned fabric artist. Clothing designer. International entrepreneur. Business owner. How many boutiques is it now?"

Clearly he'd done some homework, too.

"Seven," Ally said shortly. "I just opened one in Honolulu last month."

She had gone to California to art school after leaving Hawaii—after their marriage—and to supplement the money from her grandmother's legacy, she'd worked in a fabric store. Always interested in art, she'd managed to put the two together rather quickly and had begun to design quilts and wall hangings that had caught the public's eye.

From there she had branched out into clothing design and creating one-of-a-kind outfits. "Art you can wear," she'd called it.

Now her work was featured not only in her own shops, but in galleries and even a few textile museums all over the world.

"Impressive," PJ said now. He balanced one ankle on the opposite knee.

"I worked hard," she said firmly. " You knew I would. You saw that I had." Five years ago, she meant.

"I did," he agreed, lounging back in his chair, and regarding her intently as he drawled, "And you didn't need any more favors from me."

Ally stiffened. But she knew that from his perspective she was the one who had been out of line. "I was rude to you that night."

It had been the last time—the *only* time—she had seen PJ since the day of their marriage.

She'd come back to Honolulu for her first local public art show. It had been in the heady scary early days of her career when she certainly hadn't been a "household name" or anything close. In fact the show itself had doubtless been premature, but she'd wanted desperately to do it, to prove to her father that she was on her way to making something of herself, and—though she'd barely admitted to herself—she'd hoped to see PJ, too, to show him that his faith in her had not been misplaced. So she'd jumped at the chance to be part of the show when another artist backed out.

She'd sent her father an invitation to the opening and had waited with nervous pride and anticipation for his arrival.

He'd never come.

But PJ had.

Looking up all of a sudden to see him there across the room, big as life and twice as gorgeous as she remembered, had knocked Ally for a loop.

She hadn't expected to see him at all.

When she'd known she was coming back, she'd casually asked a friend who had gone to the same beach with them about where PJ was now.

May had shaken her head. "PJ? No idea. Haven't seen him in ages. But you know surfers—they never stay. They're always following the waves."

So the sight of him had been a shock. As had the sight of the woman on his arm.

She was, in a blonde bombshell way, every bit as gorgeous as PJ himself. With his dark hair and tan and her platinum tresses and fair skin, the contrast between the two was eye-catching and arresting. The artist in Ally had certainly appreciated that.

The woman in her didn't appreciate him striding up to her, all smiles, hugging her and saying cheerfully, "Hey. Look at you! You look great. And your stuff—" he let go of her to wave an arm around the gallery "—looks great, too. Amazing. I brought you a reviewer." He'd introduced the blonde then, took her arm and pulled her forward. "This is Annie Cannavaro. She writes art reviews for the *Star*."

He had not said, "This is Ally, my wife."

In fact, he hadn't mentioned any relationship to her at all. Not that Ally had expected him to. She knew their marriage had been for her convenience, not a lifelong commitment. He'd done her a favor.

But standing there, being introduced to the *Star*'s art critic, made her realize that PJ thought she needed another favor now. The very thought had made her see red. She was not still the needy girl she'd been when he married her!

He'd been perplexed at her brusqueness. But Ally had been too insecure still to accept his freely offered help.

And—a truth she acknowledged to no one, barely even to herself—seeing PJ with another woman, a far more suitable woman for him than she was, had made it a thousand times worse.

She'd been stiff and tense and had determinedly feigned indifference all the time they were there. And she'd only breathed a sigh of relief when she'd seen them go out the door. Her relief, though, had been short-lived.

Right before closing, PJ had returned. Alone.

He'd cornered her in one of the gallery rooms, demanding, "What the hell is wrong with you?" His normally easygoing smile was nowhere to be found.

"I don't know what you're talking about," she'd replied frostily, trying to sidestep and get around him, but he moved to block her exit.

"You know damned well what I'm talking about. So you don't want to know me, okay. Maybe you're too much of a hotshot now. Fine, but that's no reason to be rude to Annie."

"I wasn't! I'm not—a hotshot." Her face had burned furiously. She'd been mortified at his accusation. "I just…I didn't mean to be rude. I just don't need your help. You don't need to keep rescuing me!"

"I'm not bloody rescuing you," he'd snapped. "I thought you'd like the exposure. But if that's the way you see it, fine. I'll tell her not to write anything!"

"You can tell her what to write?" So it was true!

He'd said a rude word. "Forget it. Sorry I bothered." He spun away and started out of the room.

But she couldn't let him go without calling after him, "Is that all?"

He looked over his shoulder. "All? What else could there be?"

Ally's mouth was dry. She had to force the words out. "I thought...I thought you'd be bringing the divorce papers." She'd feared there was a quaver in her voice, but she tried not to betray it.

PJ stared at her. She met his gaze even though it was the hardest thing she'd ever done.

"No," he said at last, his voice flat. "I don't have any divorce papers."

"Oh." And there was no accounting for the foolish shiver of relief she'd felt.

Still they'd stared at each other, and then she'd dragged in a breath and shrugged. "Fine. Well, I just thought...whenever you want one, just let me know." She'd tried to sound blasé and indifferent.

"Yeah," PJ said. "I'll do that." And he'd turned and walked away.

She hadn't seen him again, hadn't heard from him, hadn't contacted him—until today.

Now she said carefully, "I apologize for that. I was still trying to find my own way. I'd depended on you enough. I didn't want another handout."

"Is that what it was?" There was a rough edge to his voice. The cool irony of his earlier words was past.

Their gazes locked—and held—and something seemed to arc between them like an electric current.

Or rather, Ally assured herself, more like a sparkler on the Fourth of July—bright and fizzing, ultimately insubstantial—and definitely best ignored.

Determinedly she gave her head a little shake. "I'm sure that's what it was," she said firmly. "I shouldn't have done it, though. Anyway, I've found out who I am and what I can do. And I owe it to you. So I came to say thank you belatedly and—" she reached down and picked up the portfolio she had set by her chair and opened it just as she'd rehearsed doing "—to bring you these."

She slid a file of papers out of the portfolio and held it out to him.

He took the file, looked at it, but didn't open it. "What are they?"

"Divorce papers. About time, huh?" She said it quickly, then shrugged and grinned as brightly as she could, willing him to grin back at her.

He didn't. His gaze fixed on the file in his hand, weighing it, but he didn't say a word.

"I know I should have done it sooner," she went on, papering over the awkward silence. "I'm sorry it took so long. I thought you'd do it. You could have had one at any time, you know. Well, almost anytime. After I turned twenty-one anyway. I told you so, remember?"

He still didn't speak. He didn't even blink. His face was stony, his expression unreadable. And so she babbled on, unable to help herself. "I know it's past time. I should have taken care of it ages ago. It's a formality really—just confirming what we already know. I don't want anything from you, of course. No settlement, naturally. But," she added because she'd already decided this, "if you want a share of my business, it's yours. You're entitled."

"I don't." The words cut across hers, harsh and louder than she expected.

"Well, I wanted to offer." She took a breath. "Okay, then it will be even easier." She reached inside her portfolio for a pen. "In that case, all you really need to do is sign them. I can take care of the rest."

"I don't think so."

The rough edge was gone now. PJ's voice was smooth and cool, like an ocean breeze. Ally looked up, startled.

He was sitting up straight in the chair and was regarding her steadily.

"Well, of course I'll understand if you want a lawyer to look them over...." Still she fumbled for the pen.

"I don't." Still cool. Very cool.

She frowned, rattled. "Well then—" Her fingers fastened on the pen at last. She jerked it out and thrust it at him, giving him one more quick smile. "Here you go."

He didn't move. Didn't take it.

And of course, she realized then, he didn't need one. He already had a pen in his shirt pocket. She felt like an idiot as she gestured toward it. "Of course you have your own."

But he didn't get it out. Instead PJ dropped the papers on the table, then looked up and met her gaze squarely. "No divorce."

CHAPTER TWO

"WHAT? What do you mean, no divorce?"

"Seems pretty clear to me. Which word didn't you understand?" He raised an eyebrow.

Ally stared at him, unable to believe her ears. "Ha-ha. Very funny. Come on, PJ. You've had your joke. You made your point. I was rude. I'm sorry. I've grown up, changed. Now just sign the papers and I'll be on my way."

"I don't think so."

"Why not?" She was rattled now. "It doesn't make any sense."

"Sure it does." He shrugged. "We're married. We took vows."

"Oh, yes, right. And we've certainly kept them, haven't we?"

The brow lifted again and he said mildly, "Speak for yourself, Al."

She gaped at him. "What are you saying?"

"Never mind." He looked away out the window, stared out at Manhattan across the river for a long moment while Ally stewed, waiting for him to enlighten her. Finally he looked her way again. "I'm just saying we've been married for ten years. That's a long time. Lots of marriages don't last that long," he added.

"Are you suggesting that more people shouldn't see each other for ten years? Or five," she added, forcing herself to add that one disastrous meeting.

He shook his head, smiling slightly. "No. I'm saying we should give it a shot."

"What?" She couldn't believe her ears. "Give what a shot?"

"Marriage. Living together. Seeing if it will work." Deep green eyes bored into hers.

Ally opened her mouth, then closed it again. She couldn't believe this was happening. Not now! Not ever, for that matter. That had never been the plan. Not for her, and certainly not for PJ.

"We don't know each other," she pointed out.

"We were friends once."

"You were a beach bum and I was the counter girl where you bought plate lunches and hamburgers."

"We met there," he agreed. "And we became friends. You're not trying to say we weren't friends."

"No." She couldn't say that. They had been friends. "But that's the point. We were *friends*, PJ. Buddies. We never even went out! You certainly didn't love me then! And you can't possibly love me now."

"So? I like what I see. And a lot of marriages start with less."

He made it sound eminently sensible and reasonable—as if it were perfectly logical for two people to go their separate ways for ten years and then suddenly, without warning, pick up where they left off.

Maybe to him it was. After all, he'd married her with no real forethought at all. It had been useful to her, so he had done it.

She shook her head. "That's ridiculous."

"No, it's not."

"Of course it is. We don't live anywhere near each other. We have entirely different lives."

"I'm adaptable."

"Well, I'm not! I've got a life in Hawaii now. I've come home, settled down. I like it there. I've worked hard to get where I am, to do what I'm doing. It's time to take the next step."

"Which is?"

"Get a divorce!"

"No."

"Yes! I've got to," she said. "I...I'm getting a life!"

"Finally?" His tone was mocking.

She wrapped her arms across her chest. "I had other things to do first. You know that."

"And now you've done them, so you want a divorce." A brow lifted. "Why now?"

"Because I've found you, for one thing," she said with a touch of annoyance. "And why wait? It's not as if we've got a relationship. On the contrary, we have nothing."

"We have memories."

"Ten-year-old memories," she scoffed.

"And one five-year-old one," PJ reminded her.

Ally's face burned. "I've apologized for that!"

"So you have. Thank you," he said formally. "Anyway, it's not my fault we didn't keep in touch," he pointed out. "You're the one who didn't leave a forwarding address."

"Mea culpa," Ally muttered. But then she added, "Maybe I should have kept in touch, but—"

But doing so would have been a temptation she didn't want to have to deal with. Marrying PJ had been one thing—it had been a few words recited, a couple of signatures scrawled. It had been a legal document, but it hadn't been personal. Not really.

That night, though—that one night with PJ—had destroyed all her notions of their marriage being no more than an impersonal business proposition. It had made her want things she knew she had no business wanting, things she was sure PJ definitely didn't want. She knew he'd married her to help her out.

To change the rules after the fact wouldn't have been fair.

She shook her head. "I just thought it was better if I didn't."

"No distractions," PJ translated flatly.

"Yes," Ally lied. "But times change. People change as you said." She gave him the brightest smile she could manage under the circumstances, but she couldn't quite meet his eyes.

"So what's the real reason, Al?"

The question cut across the jumble of her thoughts exactly

the way his suggestion that he marry her had cut across the morass of worries she'd wallowed in all those years ago.

She hadn't counted on that, any more than she'd counted on this.

She'd assured herself that seeing PJ again would be a good thing. That it was the right thing to do—the polite thing to do—come and ask him face-to-face to sign the divorce papers rather than simply mail the papers to him.

She'd been convinced that seeing him again would bring closure.

She'd convinced herself that she would walk into PJ's office and have changed enough to feel nothing more than gratitude to the man she had married ten years before.

And even if she'd still felt a twinge of regret, she'd been sure he would be delighted to comply with her request. After all, being married to her was holding up his life, too. With the papers signed, they would go their own ways and that would be that.

Now she watched as PJ took a sip of tea and cocked his head, waiting for her answer.

"I'm getting married," she said at last.

PJ choked. "What?"

"I said, I'm getting married. Not everyone considers me a charity case," she said sharply. His eyes narrowed, but she plunged on. "I'm…engaged. Sort of."

"Isn't that a little…precipitous? You already have one husband."

"It's not official," she said. "It's just…going to happen. After. Which is why I brought the divorce papers. So you could sign them. It's a formality really. I could have sent them by mail. I just thought it was more polite to bring them in person."

"Polite," he echoed. His tone disputed her assertion.

"I am polite," she defended herself. "I didn't imagine you'd have any interest in…keeping things going. It's not as if we've ever had a real marriage."

"We did for one night."

Her teeth came together with a snap. "That wasn't...real."

"Felt pretty real to me."

"Stop it! You know what I mean!"

He sighed. "Tell me what you mean, Al."

"I mean it's time to move on. I should have done something sooner. Contacted you sooner. But I thought you would...and then five years ago, I was sure you would...and then I just...got busy. And after I came back to Honolulu, I wasn't sure where you were and I didn't think it mattered and then things got...serious. Jon...proposed and..."

"He didn't know you were married?"

"He knew I *was*. I guess he thought it was in the past," she added awkwardly. How did you tell someone you were seeing that you still had a husband, you just didn't know where?

"And you didn't bother to set him straight?"

"It never came up."

PJ's eyes widened. "Really?" Patent disbelief.

"We didn't spend a lot of time talking about it!" she snapped. "What was there to say? He said he'd heard about my marriage from his brother and I said yes. There was nothing else. He, well, he assumed it was over. And I...said it was."

PJ raised an eyebrow.

"Well, it has been—in everything but the formalities. It never even really got started!"

"Oh, I think you could say it got started, Al." The look he gave her reminded her all too well of the night that had been anything but platonic.

"It was one night!"

But what a night. Especially for a wedding night that wasn't supposed to have happened at all.

Making love with PJ hadn't been part of the deal—the original deal. She'd never intended to consummate their marriage. And PJ had never mentioned it, either.

But after the ceremony, when she'd gone home to tell her father she was married, he had just stared at her and, after what seemed an eternity, he said, "You're married?" Even longer pause. "Really?"

And long after he'd walked away from her, those two words had still echoed in her head.

Was it a marriage? Was saying words and scrawling signatures enough to make it a marriage? Or was there more to it than that?

Of course there was. Ally had always known that.

She'd seen the deep love of her parents. She'd witnessed the shattering pain her father had felt at her mother's death. Her marriage to PJ, in that light, was a sham indeed.

And while she knew ultimately why they had married, she felt compelled by her father's doubt and, even more, by her own convictions, to want a "real marriage" with PJ Antonides.

And so that night she had gone to PJ's apartment.

She could still remember the incredulity on his face when he had opened the door and found her standing there. "Ally? What's up?"

"I..." She'd swallowed hard. "I need another favor."

"Yeah, sure, name it." He'd shrugged, still looking at her strangely because, of course, he hadn't expected to see her at all.

Her fingers had twisted together, strangled each other, as she looked up into his eyes. "Could you, um, please make love to me?"

He'd looked at her, stunned. And for so long, that she'd been tempted to turn tail and run. She'd tried to explain. "I know why you married me. I know you're doing me a favor, putting your name on a piece of paper, But I...I just want it to be real!"

He didn't move. Didn't blink. Just stared.

"I know making love doesn't make it 'real'—not like other marriages," she said hastily. "And I know it won't happen again. I just thought—if you wanted..." Her voice trailed off. "Maybe you don't find me attractive. I understand. I—"

"Don't be stupid," PJ said harshly. He grasped her hand and drew her in.

And Ally's breath caught in her throat. "I don't expect—"

"Shh," PJ's voice was a whisper, a breath—that began on his lips and ended on hers.

The touch of his mouth, warm and persuasive against hers, made Ally's legs weak, made her mind spin, made her clutch his arms, then wrap hers around his back and hang on for dear life as he pushed the door shut behind her and steered her to his bed without ever breaking their kiss.

And then he made love to her.

Ally had expected it to be quick and uncomfortable and perfunctory—one coupling to make their marriage "real." And, because she supposed that PJ would enjoy sex, she'd considered that to be the one small thing she could give him.

As far as she went, as a virgin, Ally had no real experience to draw on. And everything she'd heard had made "first times" sound something to be endured rather than enjoyed.

On the contrary, PJ had made it the most amazing night of her life.

Making love with PJ, sharing intimacies with PJ she'd never shared with anyone, had been such an incredible experience that she had never been able to forget it. She hadn't wanted to.

There had been nothing quick or perfunctory about it. PJ had been gentle and thorough, touching and caressing her in ways that made her ache with longing for him. His gentleness had made her want to weep at the same time it had made her exult with the joy of finding out what her body was all about.

And if there had been a bit of discomfort the first time, it was nothing in the face of the concern PJ expressed, his determination to make it good for her, too. And he had. All night he had.

If she hadn't been already half in love with PJ Antonides, she certainly would have been by the next morning. Not that she could tell him so. That, too, would have been changing the rules.

But it didn't stop her thinking about him. Didn't stop her loving him from afar. Didn't stop her reliving those memories. They were memories she'd lived on for years.

For a long time those memories had made her doubt that she would ever be able to look at another man.

The fact was, she hadn't really looked at another man until she'd met Jon.

And she still had no idea if it would be the same with Jon as it had been with PJ. She hadn't wanted to find out. She hadn't made love with Jon.

"I can't," she'd told him firmly when she'd also told him that she was legally still PJ's wife. "I can't make love with one man when I'm still married to another."

"I admire your scruples," Jon had muttered. "Get the damn divorce so we can get married, then."

And so she was.

She loved Jon. In his way he was exactly what she wanted and needed—a kind man, a caring man. A man who wanted a wife and a family. A man who was tired of being a workaholic, just as she was.

"We're good for each other," Jon had said not long ago. "We want the same things."

They did. Something she and PJ had never done. Would never do. They wanted different things. As soon as the divorce was final, she was going to marry Jon, make a life with him. And she was going to have children with him. She was going to give her father the grandchild he longed for.

And she would make new memories, wonderful ones that would supercede those of one night in PJ's arms.

"It was a deal we made," she told PJ firmly now. "It was never a real marriage."

"It was," he said. "And you know it."

She'd thought so then, but now she shook her head. "I was immature. Marriage is a lot more than one night in bed."

"Of course it is. But it's all we had. You left."

"Would you have wanted me to stay?" she challenged. "I don't think so! You didn't want a marriage then, PJ, and don't pretend you did! You wanted to surf and cut class and hang around on the beach. You know that." She glared at him, defying him to contradict her.

His lips pressed together. And he didn't speak for such a long time that Ally found herself sitting on the edge of her chair, wondering if he might actually do that.

But then he shrugged lightly. "You're right."

She let out a harsh breath, deflated and relieved at the same time. "Of course I'm right."

But even knowing that, her gaze locked with his. And Ally couldn't help it. She found herself once more remembering the night, the tenderness, the passion, the emotion, the unexpected intimacy—and how very real it had felt.

PJ cleared his throat and looked away. He took a long swallow of his iced tea and said briskly, "So who's the lucky guy?"

"You remember Ken? That guy my dad wanted me to marry..."

"Oh, for God's sake, Ally." The words exploded from him. "You're not going to marry him!"

"No, of course not! I'm not going to marry him! He's already married. He has three kids. But he also has a younger brother. Jon's a doctor."

"A doctor." The words dropped like stones into a pond.

"A cardiologist," Ally clarified. "Very well respected. Not my dad's doctor, but in the same practice. I met him when he was filling in on rounds and came to see my dad. We hit it off. We like the same things. We want the same things."

"And so you're going to marry him? Just like that?" PJ's tone was scathing.

"I married you 'just like that'! A whole lot faster, in fact."

His mouth twisted. "For ulterior motives," he reminded her. "Do you have ulterior motives this time, Al?"

"No!"

"So you're in love with him?"

"Of course I'm in love with him!" she said quickly. "He's a wonderful man. Hardworking. Intelligent. Clever. He cares about people. Tries to heal them. To give them a new lease on life. He respects me and what I've accomplished. I respect him. It's a good match. And it's the right time for both of us. We both want a home, a family, children. I don't want my family to be just Dad and me. Neither does my father. He's over the moon about Jon."

"I'll bet."

She bristled at his tone. "I'd marry him even if Dad didn't like him. Jon is a great guy."

"Which doesn't change the fact that you're still married to me."

And there they were—back at the divorce papers again. The divorce papers PJ wasn't signing. The divorce papers that were sitting on the table between them. The divorce papers that even now he refused to look at. And Ally knew from the stubborn jut of his jaw—the same one she'd seen when he'd been determined to ride waves in surf sane men back away from—that he wasn't going to change his mind now.

She let out a breath and stood up. "Fine. You don't have to sign them." She picked up her portfolio. "I can do it without your consent."

A muscle ticked in his cheek, but he didn't answer, just looked at her.

She plucked her business card out of the portfolio and tossed it on top of the divorce papers. "Really, PJ, I—"

But his expression was entirely shuttered. Okay, so she'd been wrong to come. Jon had been right when she'd told him where she was going. If he'd been taken aback that she was still married, he'd been even more upset at her notion of coming to see PJ and giving him the papers in person.

"Don't open a can of worms," he'd said. "You could get hurt."

But she'd insisted it was the right thing to do. PJ had done her a favor once. The least she could do was say thank you when they ended their marriage.

At least, that had been the plan.

Now she said to PJ, "Call me if you change your mind. I'll be in the city until Friday. Otherwise, I'll see you in court."

* * *

"You do have a wife."

"I said I did," PJ replied sharply.

It wasn't news. He'd never said otherwise. It wasn't his fault no one believed him. They'd always treated his assertion as if it were a joke.

It wasn't a joke.

Or if it was, the joke was on him.

Sometimes he thought that his marriage to Ally was more like a dream—a distant recollection of one moment out of his life that seemed to have no connection to the rest of his life, except for one, which had ended badly.

He should have left it there. Or filed for divorce himself after their set-to at the gallery five years ago.

But he hadn't. Why bother?

He'd certainly had no intention of marrying at the time. In fact having a wife in absentia had actually been convenient. He'd had a built-in reason for never getting serious. It had stood him in good stead in Hawaii back in his beach-bum days. But it had been even more of a godsend since he'd come back to New York and his parents had begun dragging out every available woman they knew.

"Don't bother," he'd said straight off. "I'm married."

They hadn't believed him, of course.

Where was his wife? *Who* was his wife? They'd dismissed it as a joke, too, until he'd shown them the marriage license.

Then they'd had a thousand questions, each nosier and more personal than the last. He'd only answered the ones he wanted to. He'd told them her name, where he'd met her, why he'd married her.

"A favor?" his father had sputtered. "You married her for a favor?"

"Why not?" PJ had said flatly, folding his arms across his chest. "She was between a rock and a hard place. She needed a way out. You'd have done the same," he said bluntly. His father, for all his bombast, was a far bigger softie than any of his children. "Wouldn't you?" he'd challenged the old man.

Aeolus had grunted.

"So when is she coming back?" he and Helena had both wanted to know.

"When she finds herself," PJ had replied. That was probably the closest he'd come to telling a lie.

How the hell did he know when or what Ally would do? He'd have thought she'd be glad to see him when he'd turned up at her gallery opening. Instead she'd been stiff and remote and defensive.

She hadn't even seemed like Ally. She'd been dismissive of Annie, completely misunderstanding his reason for bringing the other woman along. She hadn't seemed at all like the girl he'd married. He'd told himself it didn't matter, that he should just forget her.

But he couldn't. She was always there—Ally and the one night they'd shared.

"You should go get her," *Yiayia* told him. *Yiayia* was always full of ideas. The minute word of PJ's marriage had come to her ears, she'd been busy figuring out how to bring them together again.

"No." PJ was adamant. "Things are fine just the way they are."

If he'd hoped they would be different, if now and then he had even begun to think about how to make them different, it wasn't something he'd spent a lot of time dwelling on. Nor was he going to discuss it with *Yiayia*.

"Pah," *Yiayia* had said. "What good is a wife when she is not here? It is not good for a man to be alone, Petros. And it is not good for a great-grandmother to be denied her rightful great-grandchildren, either."

He'd glowered at her. "That's what this is all about really," he'd grumbled.

"Do you think so?" *Yiayia* said. Then she'd shaken her head in dismay. "You are hiding behind her skirts."

"I am not! How the hell can I hide behind the skirts of someone who isn't even here."

"You use her not to deal with the women your father brings you."

PJ shrugged. "I don't want them."

"Because you want her."

"That's not true!"

"So prove it. Not to me." *Yiayia* cut off his protest before he could open his mouth. "For yourself. Go find her. See what she is like now. Bring her home. Or get a divorce."

He ground his teeth, but *Yiayia* just looked at him serenely. Finally he'd shrugged. "Maybe I will."

"'Maybe' builds no fires to keep me warm. 'Maybe' gives me no great-grandbabies."

"Fine, damn it," he said, goaded. "It's our tenth anniversary in August. I'll track her down. Take her out to dinner to celebrate."

And sort things out once and for all.

Yiayia smiled and patted his knee. "Bring her home to meet us. It is good she meets your family, *ne*, Petros?"

PJ hadn't answered that. But he knew she was right about one thing.

He was thirty-two years old now. Not twenty-two, or even twenty-seven. He was ready to be married to someone who was actually present in his life. And though some of the women his father turned up with were actually quite nice, he still hadn't forgotten Ally.

And now Ally was back.

"She's gorgeous," Rosie said now.

"Yeah."

In fact, gorgeous didn't cover the half of it. Ally had always been amazing looking. He'd been struck by that the first time he'd seen her behind the counter at Benny's taking orders.

The combined genes of her Japanese father and her Chinese-Hawaiian-Anglo mother had come together to make Alice

Maruyama an absolute beauty with a porcelain complexion, high cheekbones beneath wide slightly tilted dark eyes, with the longest eyelashes he'd ever seen.

Her shining black hair had always been neatly tamed, nicely brushed, pinned down or pulled up.

Except for the night he'd made love to her. And then it had been a lavish black silk curtain, loose and lush, that begged him to thread it through his fingers, bury his face in it, rub his cheek against it.

The second she'd walked through the door this afternoon, his fingers had itched to undo that sleek librarian's knot at the back of head, let down her hair and do all those things again.

Good thing he had a well-honed sense of self-preservation. Good thing he'd learned something from going to see her at her gallery opening wearing his heart on his sleeve. He'd been a fool for her once. He wasn't doing it again.

But he wasn't letting her walk blithely away, either.

There was still something between them. Electricity. Attraction. Unfinished business.

Had she ever spent a night like their wedding night with bloody Jon? His fingers balled into fists at the thought.

How could she just walk in here and toss divorce papers at him? Why should she want to marry another man?

What the hell was wrong with the one she had?

And how could she be sure their marriage wouldn't work if they'd never even tried?

"—wants you to call her." Rosie's voice cut through his irritated thoughts. "She called while your, um, wife was with you."

PJ's thoughts jerked back to the present. "Who? What?"

Rosie gave him a long-suffering look. "Cristina," she repeated patiently. "Your sister?" she added when he didn't respond. "She said Mark just got back from San Diego and wants to discuss that new powerboat line he's been looking at so she wondered if you'd like to come to dinner."

Dinner. Cristina. Mark.

PJ dragged his brain back to business, determinedly putting Ally on a sidebar long enough to make sense of what Rosie was telling him.

His twin sister Cristina's husband, Mark, worked for Antonides Marine as well. They had a brownstone not far from his place in Park Slope and sometimes it was easier to talk business over the dinner table than in the office. It was, after all, a family business.

Ally wanted family. She'd said so. She didn't just want it to be her and her father anymore. She'd said that, too.

Well, hell, PJ thought, cracking his knuckles. If Ally wanted family, he had more than enough to go around.

"Call Cristina back and tell her I can't make it," he instructed Rosie. "Tell her I'll catch Mark in the office tomorrow." He smiled a cat-who'd-eaten-the-canary smile. "Tell her I'm busy tonight. I'm fixing dinner for my wife."

"So, did you get it?" Jon asked.

"Not yet," Ally said, pacing around her hotel room. She hadn't wanted to call without things being settled, but when they didn't she knew she had to call anyway. She just hoped she didn't have to listen to Jon say, I told you so. "I will," she promised, but it didn't forestall the discussion.

"Didn't you go see him? I thought you knew where he was."

"I do know where he is," she said. "I saw him. And I will get it. I just didn't…think it was right to waltz back into his life and fling divorce papers at him first thing."

"I knew this was a bad idea."

"It was not a bad idea," Ally retorted. "He was surprised."

"To see you or to get the papers?"

"Well, both, I guess. Don't worry. I'm sure he'll sign them. PJ doesn't react well to pressure."

She should have remembered that. Should have recalled

why he'd said he'd come to Hawaii in the first place: to get his family off his back.

She should have been less...pushy. She should have simply chatted with him, got him to talk, acted interested in what he was doing now, what had happened to him in the past ten years, how he'd come to be where he was and doing what he was doing.

The trouble was—and the very reason she didn't do it was—that it wouldn't have been an act.

She had gone to PJ's office hoping that their encounter would be polite and perfunctory. In a best-case scenario she would have felt no more connection to him than she had to Jon's brother, Ken.

She would certainly *not* have felt an instant stab of lust and longing. Her eyes would not have fastened on PJ's well-dressed body and lingered, cataloguing every inch of it. And they would definitely not have mentally undressed that body while her brain wondered as they did so how the man in the suit would compare with the naked twenty-two-year-old she had spent her wedding night with.

Not something she should be contemplating now, either.

"So when?" Jon asked. "I'll be having dinner with your dad tonight. He'll want to know. I was hoping to be able to tell him it was a done deal and you were on your way home."

"I won't be home until the weekend. You both know that. I'm going to be visiting a gallery here, too, talking to Gabriela, the owner. This trip wasn't all about PJ."

"No. It's about *us*," Jon reminded her. "It's about you finally putting the past behind you and moving on. You are moving on, aren't you, Ally?"

"Of course I am."

"Well, I'm only saying...your dad's heart isn't strong. It's not going to hold out forever. And I know you—and I—wanted him to be at our wedding."

Ally swallowed against the lump in her throat. Yes, she did know her father's condition was delicate. And she knew how happy seeing her married to Jon would make him. And she did want him to be happy. She wanted them all to be happy.

"I'm working on it."

"Good. I'll tell him that. Then hurry up and get home. I miss you. I work twenty hours a day when you're not here."

Ally knew the feeling. "I'll do my best," she promised. "I'm getting another call. It might be Gabriela. I'd better take it."

"Forget Gabriela. Forget the gallery. They aren't that important. Not now. Get the papers signed."

"Yes. Maybe this is PJ," Ally suggested hopefully. "Maybe he's already signed them and is telling me when to pick them up."

"Let's hope." Jon sounded encouraged. "Talk to you tomorrow. I'll tell your dad you've got everything under control."

Ally hoped it was true. She punched the connect button on her phone. "This is Alice Maruyama."

"Have dinner with me." The voice was gruff and male and needed no identification.

She'd heard it only an hour before, but if she hadn't heard PJ Antonides's voice for ten years, she would have recognized it. There was a sort of soft, lazy, sexy edge to it that made her toes curl.

"Who is this?" she said with all the starch she could muster.

He laughed. "Check your caller ID. Come on, Al. Don't be a bad sport. You never used to be a bad sport."

"This has nothing to do with sports. It has to do with you signing the divorce papers."

"So convince me over dinner."

"PJ…"

"Are you chicken, Al? Afraid?" It was the same old taunt he'd used years ago. In the same teasing tone.

When she had met him she'd never surfed in her life, and he'd been appalled.

"Never surfed? And you live where?" He'd stared at her, stunned. She'd just handed him his order from the lunch counter and expected him to move along, but he stayed right where he was, ignoring the line behind him.

"Not everyone who lives in Hawaii surfs," she'd said haughtily.

He'd shrugged. "Guess not," he'd agreed. Then he'd slanted her a grin. "And why should you if you're chicken?"

"I'm not chicken!"

"Then come out with me," he'd suggested. "I'll teach you."

"I have work to do." She'd waved her arm around, pointing out the fact that she had responsibilities, even if he didn't. "I can't just walk out and go play with you."

"So come tomorrow morning. Better surf then anyway. I'll meet you here at seven." He'd tipped his head, the slow grin still lingering, green eyes dancing. "Unless you're—"

"I am *not* chicken!" Ally said it then. She said it again now. "Fine. I'll have dinner with you. We can catch up on 'old times.' And you can sign the papers. Where shall I meet you?"

"I'll pick you up."

"I'd rather meet you there."

He paused, then said, "Fine. Suit yourself." He gave her a street corner in Brooklyn. "You can take a cab or the subway. Either way, I'll meet you at the Seventh Avenue subway stop."

"I'll go to the restaurant."

"I'll be at the subway stop. We can walk from there. Seven o'clock. It's a date."

CHAPTER THREE

IT WAS *not* a date.

Ally had never been on a date with PJ Antonides in her life—unless you counted their date to meet at the courthouse where they got married, which she wasn't, she thought irritably, jerking clothes out of her suitcase, trying to find something suitable to wear.

Not that it mattered. It wasn't a date, despite what he had said. And they weren't a couple!

She was annoyed. With PJ. But even more with herself. And even more that she was annoyed and had let him get to her.

She was kicking herself now for having done the polite thing and come to give him the papers in person. Jon was right. She hadn't needed to. She could have sent them through the mail. And if he hadn't signed them, oh, well. She'd have proceeded with the divorce anyway.

Of course, she still could. But it was worse now, having stirred the pot, so to speak. And she couldn't understand why he was being obstinate. She'd thought her task would be simple.

She'd expected that PJ would be delighted to see her, that he would tease her a bit—as he always had done—then, still joking with her, he'd sign the papers, maybe buy her a cup of coffee, then give her a wink and a wave as she walked out the door.

Her only qualm about seeing him again had been wondering what her own reaction would be.

PJ had turned her world upside down the night he'd made love to her. He had made her want things she hadn't suspected existed—things that she'd tried to put out of her mind ever since.

Worse, he had made her want him.

And, on a physical level, her body still did.

Which was why she was putting on a tailored black pantsuit and knotting her hair up on top of her head—tamping down and buttoning up—to remind herself that this was not about physical desire.

It was about commitment and family and eternity.

It was about ending their sham of a marriage so that she could move on and make a real one with Jon.

"Just remember that," she told her reflection, staring intently into her dark eyes and willing herself to be strong. "PJ doesn't love you. He's just getting his own back."

She was fairly sure that was what this reluctance was all about. He was making her pay, no doubt, for having been rude and distant the night he'd come to her opening.

"He doesn't love you," she repeated once more for good measure, then added severely, "and you don't love him, either."

The subway ride from her midtown Manhattan hotel to the Seventh Avenue stop in Brooklyn wilted her pantsuit. A straphanger's charm bracelet snagged her hair. She was disheveled, unkempt and perspiring by the time she emerged onto the street. She wished he'd told her what restaurant they were going to so she could have gone there and repaired the damage before she met him again.

But he was already there waiting when she appeared. He was still wearing the trousers and shirt he'd worn at work. His jacket was slung over his shoulder. His tie was gone. The power was still there. It was like seeing the wild animal let out of his cage.

Ally caught her breath.

"Right on time," he said approvingly. "No trouble getting here? You look great."

That was so patently a lie that Ally laughed.

He grinned. "Ah, a real smile at last."

"It's just that I'm so delighted to be here," she said sarcastically.

He laughed. And before she realized—or prepared, or dodged—he swooped around, ducked his head down and kissed her.

It was a quick kiss—a street-corner kiss. A smack of lips, an instant's worth of the taste of enticing sexy male and nothing more. It was the sort of kiss that happened every day on thousands of street corners around the world. Nothing earth-shattering about it.

At least, no one else's world shattered.

Only hers.

Because that one brief touch of PJ's lips brought everything back. The memories she'd wallowed in at first, then spent years sublimating or suppressing, crashed back in on her as if the years of constructing defenses had never even happened.

That one instant, that one taste—his lips on hers, his scent filling her nostrils—and for a split second she was back in Hawaii, back in PJ's apartment, back in his arms.

She swayed, stumbled.

He caught her before she could fall on her face. "Are you okay?"

Of course she was, but he kept his arm around her as she wobbled on knees of jelly. And she gripped his shirtfront as she righted herself, then let go as she straightened and pulled away. "I'm fine. It's the heat. And...and I just t-tripped, that's all."

"You sure?" He was so close. She could see each individual eyelash. They were long and thick and wasted on a man. He bent close again, looking worried and solicitous.

Ally stepped back quickly, out of kissing range. Definitely out of kissing range!

"It was hot in the subway. The air-conditioning wasn't working on the train. Where are we going? Is it far? I need to splash some water on my face."

"Not far." He still had his arm around her as he steered her along Flatbush Avenue and into a grocery store.

She frowned. "Where are you going?"

"Just have to get a few things. Come on." He came back and snagged her wrist to take her with him. She pulled out of his grasp, but followed as he picked some steaks, salad vegetables, a loaf of country bread and fresh olives. Then he hesitated a moment, as if weighing his options, and grabbed a couple of ears of corn on the cob.

Suspicion began to dawn. "Why are you shopping now?"

"Because until an hour ago, I didn't know I was having company for dinner."

"We're not...I mean...*you're cooking?*"

"No end to my talents." He slanted her a grin as he grabbed a fresh pineapple off the display and tossed it to her.

Instinctively Ally caught it but protested as she did so. "You don't have to cook for me," she said quickly. "Let's go out. I'll buy dinner."

"No. You won't. Come on. No trouble at all. I like to cook."

"But—"

But he was already leading the way toward the checkout. "Hey, Manny. How's it going?" he said to the teenager who began to ring up the groceries.

"Ain't. Too hot," the boy said. "Dyin' in here. Better outside. Don't forget. Softball tonight."

"Not me. Other plans."

The boy's gaze lit on Ally and he looked her up and down assessingly. "Nice," he said with an approving grin.

"My wife," PJ said.

Ally stiffened beside him. He didn't have to keep telling everyone.

The boy was clearly surprised. His eyes widened. "No joke?"

"Yep."

"No," Ally said at the same instant.

Manny blinked. PJ's scowl was disapproving.

"Only officially," she muttered.

PJ's jaw tightened. "Officially counts." He pulled out his wallet and paid for the groceries. "Hit a homer for me."

Manny grinned and winked. "Hit one yourself."

Ally's cheeks burned as she followed PJ out of the store. "Why do you keep telling people I'm your wife?"

"Because it's the truth?" he suggested.

"But not for long." She practically had to lope to keep up with him.

"You're here now."

"Just for the night. I'm leaving Friday."

"Stop thinking so damn far ahead, Al." PJ shifted the grocery bag into his other arm and took her by the elbow as they turned the corner onto one of the side streets. His touch through the thin fabric of her jacket made her far too aware of him. And she jumped when his lips came close to her ear and said, "Interesting things can happen in a night if you let them."

"Nothing's going to happen tonight," she said firmly, "or any other," in case he had any more ideas.

PJ didn't reply. He led the way with long strides. And keeping up with them reminded her of those bright mornings on the beach when he'd been determined to teach her how to surf and she'd practically had to run to match his strides across the sand.

Just when she was about to say, Slow down, he veered over midblock and steered her up the stairs to a very elegant-looking town house.

"Here?" Ally didn't know what she'd expected, but it wasn't this.

One in a row of late nineteenth-century four-story brownstone-and-brick homes, all of which were as attractive and appealing now as she was sure they had been then. The building PJ was leading her into was a far cry from the grim studio apartment over the garage of Mrs. Chang's old stucco house.

"My brother Elias lived upstairs from the office where you were today," he told her. "Antonides Marine owns the building and he fixed up the top floor for himself. It's pretty spectacular—great view—and when he left he said I could have it. But I didn't want to. I like being away from the office. I wanted a place I felt comfortable. So I found this."

He pushed open the ornate oak-and-glass double front door. "I've got the garden floor-through—that's the ground floor front to back—not exactly wide-open spaces, but I've got a garden. There's a hint of green." He was unlocking the door to his apartment as he spoke. "And, of course, the park is just over there." He jerked his head to the west. "Coney Island Beach is at the end of the subway line. And, as you can see," he said as he turned the knob and ushered her in, "I brought a little of Hawaii back with me."

She stood, stunned, at the sight of a floor-to-ceiling mural that covered one entire wall of PJ's living room. Even more stunning was that she recognized the scene at once.

It was the beach where she'd met him viewed from above on the highway. There was Benny's Place where she had worked behind the counter. There was the surfboard shop. There were the rocks, the swimmers and sunbathers, the runners in motion at the water's edge, the surfers catching the wave of the day.

She was pulled straight across the room to look at it more closely.

"How did you— Did you paint it? It's amazing."

"Not me. Not an artistic bone in my body. But my sisters are. Martha, the younger one, did this. It's what she does. Paints murals."

Ally was enchanted. "It's…captivating. I can almost feel the breeze off the sea, smell the surf and the board wax and—"

"—and Benny's plate lunch," PJ finished with a grin.

Ally laughed because it was true. "And Benny's plate lunch," she agreed, shaking her head. "It's fantastic."

PJ nodded. "I think so. It's a good reminder. Sometimes."

Ally cocked her head. "Sometimes?"

He shrugged. "Things were simpler then. Hopes, dreams. That sort of thing." His mouth twisted wryly for a moment, but then he shrugged. "But the memories are worth it, I guess. At least, most of them."

There was a moment's silence as Ally stared at the mural and reflected on her own memories of those days.

Abruptly PJ said, "I'll get started on dinner."

He vanished before she could say another word, not that she could think of anything to say. She was too captivated by the mural—and by his house.

The furniture here was all spare dark wood and leather. Bold geometric-designed rugs dotted polished wooden floors. The walls, except for the one his sister had painted, were either exposed brick or floor-to-ceiling bookshelves.

When she'd known PJ his bookshelf had been four boards and two stacks of milk crates. And the titles, as she recalled, had run to mechanical engineering texts and the latest thrillers.

His library now was much more eclectic. The texts and thrillers were still there. But there were books on woodworking and history, some art tomes and thick historical biographies. She would have liked to explore more, but the mural drew her back. She crossed the room and studied it more closely, noticing that there were people she recognized.

"That's Tuba," she said, surprised at recognizing the small figure of an island boy carrying his board on his head as he walked toward the surf. "And Benny!" she exclaimed as she found her boss sitting, as he often did, in the shade of a tree away from the bustle of his lunch shop.

"Lots of people you know," PJ agreed.

He had shed the suit and had reappeared barefoot, wearing a pair of khaki shorts and dragging a faded red shirt over his head, then tugging it down over a hard flat midriff.

This PJ she remembered—and he could still make her catch her breath. The view of his tanned muscular belly vanished in an instant, but a single glimpse was all it took. Once Ally had seen it, she could still see it in her mind. And once again she remembered things she didn't want to remember at all.

So she swallowed and dragged her gaze back up to his face, trying to remember what she had been talking about. The mural.

Right.

"Am I in it?" She was avidly curious, but didn't want to appear as if it mattered.

"Of course."

She squinted at the beach, at Benny's. "I am?" She frowned briefly and squinted more closely at it. "Where?"

He shrugged. "Doesn't matter. Come on. I'll get dinner started. Want a beer? Glass of wine?"

"Um, wine, I think."

Ally wasn't sure she should be drinking anything. She needed her brain sharp and her wits all under control. But a glass of wine might help her relax. She didn't want to feel as uptight as she felt right now. She wanted to settle down, take a deep breath, stop making such a big deal out of this.

It wasn't a big deal, she assured herself. Just a minor bump in the road on her way to marital bliss.

She should know that there were going to be bumps in the road. It was just that in the last few years she had become accustomed to things going her way. In her work, in her life. She'd made them go her way.

But PJ wasn't quite as easy to steer in the direction she wanted him to go.

She left the mural for later, tempted but at the same time unwilling to explore it further. It spoke too much of the past and she didn't need to be thinking about the past. She needed to think about the future. So she followed PJ into the kitchen.

He was every bit as intriguing as the mural. Probably more so because he was the same, yet different. In part, he was still the man she remembered—casual, easygoing, barefoot here at home—on some level taking life as it came.

But there were obviously parts of this PJ Antonides that she didn't know at all. The man who had worn the suit and stood behind the solid teak desk wasn't a man she'd had any experience with. But he was the man who had said, "No divorce."

So that was the man she would have to deal with now.

"Right," he said. "You want some wine." He removed the cork from a bottle on the counter and poured a glass of red wine, then handed it to her.

"Thank you. You're very civil."

He raised a brow. "Why shouldn't I be?"

"You weren't exactly falling all over yourself to be civil this afternoon."

"You were a bit of a surprise this afternoon."

"And now I'm not?"

"Now…we'll see. Won't we?" There was a wealth of speculation in his tone. But he didn't challenge her, just reached in the refrigerator and snagged a beer, then popped off the top.

Ally, though, thought she needed to challenge him. "Why won't you sign the divorce papers?"

"You've got a one-track mind."

"It's what I came for."

"Not to see me?"

She flushed at the accusation. "Well, of course I'm glad to see you, but…you're right. That was my priority."

"You didn't think maybe you should get to know me a little better before you decided I wouldn't suit?"

She opened her mouth, then closed it again before she said something she'd regret.

But if she'd expected him to go on, she was out of luck. He just stared at her, waiting for an answer.

"It wasn't like that, PJ," she said finally. "I met Jon when I was at the hospital with my dad. I got to know him there. Got to see how hard he worked. How much he cared. I fell in love with him there."

He didn't say a word.

She couldn't tell what he was thinking, and not knowing made her nervous. PJ had always been open and sunny, a "what you see is what you get" sort of guy.

Not now.

She was reminded again of how little she knew of him—of why he wanted her here.

"So we'll have dinner and get to know each other again, and that will do?" she asked.

"Will it?" He took the steaks out of the butcher paper and set them on a plate, then began husking the corn.

"Stop being cryptic," she said, annoyed. "What do you want?"

"What do you think I want?"

"I don't have any idea.

"It should be obvious," he said. "Time to think. I don't move fast. I weigh all my options. And I never sign anything I haven't thought over."

"Except our marriage license."

He blinked, startled, then he laughed. "Yeah. Except that."

"It's not funny. And if you think it is, you can undo it the same way," she said impatiently.

"Too soon."

"It's been ten years! Since when is there a timetable?"

He shrugged. "I don't have one." He finished preparing the corn and, wrapping it in foil, added it to the plate, then carried it out the door to the back garden. "You're the one who has the timetable."

"Because I have a fiancé," she reminded him, dogging his footsteps.

"And a husband," he reminded her over his shoulder before lighting the grill.

It all came back to that.

Ally sighed. "Yes, all right. I know. I should have done it the other way around. My bad. Honest. But think about it, PJ. I didn't even know where you were until the article came out. Was I supposed to put my life on hold until I found you?"

"Did you look?"

"I looked there. At the beach."

"Not very eager to find me."

She'd been very eager, in fact. And disappointed that he was gone. But she'd been philosophical, too. She'd never really expected him to wait around for her. They'd made no promises.

And she wasn't admitting anything now. "I would have been happy to find you," she said politely.

He turned his back to her and put the steaks on the grill. "Oh, right."

She stared at the hard shoulders, the firm muscles beneath his shirt and felt as rejected as he'd been accusing her of doing.

"Did you?" she asked.

"Did I what?"

"Come looking for me?" Two could play that game.

He turned back to face her. "You mean after you were so glad to see me at the opening? Hell, no." The word was firm, forceful. No hesitation there.

And that hurt more, even though she'd known what the answer would be. "So you should be glad to get rid of me now."

"Guess we'll see, won't we?" He tipped his beer and took a long swallow.

"Is that why you invited me to dinner?"

"Yep."

"And what can I do to convince you?"

"Give it your best shot." A corner of his mouth lifted. "Tell me about yourself now. I know what you do. I've seen your work. I didn't have to track you down to do that," he said flatly, she supposed in case she thought he'd been interested enough to do so. "But I don't know why this sudden shift."

"What shift?"

"From fiber artist and international businesswoman to little lady in search of a family." His tone was almost sarcastic but not quite. And she thought maybe if she explained, it would help, that he'd understand.

"I was in Seattle when my dad had his heart attack. I hadn't seen him in ten years."

"Your opening—"

"He didn't come."

PJ swore. "What the hell was the matter with him?"

Ally shrugged. "He wasn't ready to let go of his views, still wasn't ready to believe I could be someone other than the woman he thought I should be then. But he was actually glad to see me when I came home."

She'd been afraid he wouldn't be. Afraid he would turn away from her and shut her out in the cold. "We talked," she told PJ, "for the first time. Not a lot. But it was a start. And I...couldn't leave after that. He was all I had. I realized how much I'd missed him. How much I missed family. Even when it was just the two of us."

PJ opened his mouth, then closed it again. He leaned back against the fence and waited for her to go on.

"It was the first time I'd stopped moving, planning, 'achieving' in years." She sipped her wine reflectively and recalled those days and weeks vividly. "Being there with him for days at a time, first at the hospital, then at home, I was forced to stop and think about what I had achieved and what was missing, and—" she shrugged "—I discovered that I wanted to be more than Alice Maruyama, fiber artist and businesswoman."

It was true. All of it. But Ally stopped, astonished that she had revealed so much. She shot a quick glance at PJ to see his reaction. He hadn't moved. His eyes were hooded but focused directly on her. He nodded, listening.

That was always the way it had been with PJ. He was also focused, always intent, always listening.

"The steaks," she said abruptly, seeing the smoke from the grill.

He turned toward them. "I'll deal with 'em. Go on."

"And we talked—my dad and I—about family. About our relationship." That had been difficult. Neither she nor her father were good at that sort of thing. "And it made me realize how much I'd missed. How much I would continue to miss if I didn't— Anyway," she said briskly, "that's when I met Jon."

"And fell in love?" PJ said. The edge was back in his voice again.

"And fell in love," Ally confirmed. "Why wouldn't I? Jon is great."

PJ flipped the steaks. He didn't reply, just concentrated on the steaks, moved the foil-wrapped corn, totally absorbed in what he was doing. So absorbed that Ally wondered if he had even heard her.

Or maybe he had no comment. That was more likely the case.

And really, beyond "Where do I sign?" what did she want him to say?

"Can I help?" she asked. "Make the salad? Set the table?"

"Why don't you make the salad. Use what I bought and whatever you want from the refrigerator. Stick the bread in the oven, too, will you? Then it will be ready when the steaks are."

Grateful for something to keep herself occupied, Ally hurried back into the kitchen. Like the living room and the dining area she'd passed through on the way, it had walls of exposed brick, too. The cabinets were a light oak, the appliances stainless steel. They were all a far cry from the apartment-size stove and bar-size fridge he'd had on Oahu, and despite her insistence that she just wanted his signature and then she would be out of his life, she found that she was curious about how he lived, who he'd become.

She set about making the salad, periodically glancing back at PJ, who stood silently watching over the steaks. On one level it seemed so natural, so mundane—a husband and wife making supper at the end of a day.

On the other, to be casually cooking dinner with PJ Antonides, as if they were a simple married couple, seemed almost surreal.

She finished the salad and put it on the table, then opened the cupboards looking for plates. His kitchen was rather spare but reasonably well equipped. Obviously he was no stranger to cooking. Did he do it often? Did he have girlfriends who came and cooked for him?

A vision of Annie Cannavaro flashed through her head.

She'd told him about Jon, but he hadn't said a word about the women in his life. The newspaper article had made it clear that there were plenty of them. No one special, though?

Would he tell her if she asked?

She didn't get a chance. When he came back with the steaks a few minutes later, he said, "So tell me about how you got started with the fabric art. I remember you made some funky stuff back in the 'old days,' but I was surprised when you turned it into your profession."

She wondered if he was going to have another dig at her for her behavior at the opening in Honolulu. But he seemed actually interested, and so she explained. "When I was in California and I got a job in a fabric store while I was going to school, it seemed like something to explore further. I had access to stuff I didn't ordinarily have. So I got to try things. Experiment, you know."

He put a steak on her plate and one on his, then unwrapped the corn from the foil and added an ear to each of their plates. She dished up the salad, then cut the bread. He refilled her wineglass and got himself another beer. They sat down. "Right. Experimenting. I did that with the windsurfer. I know what you mean. Go on. I'm listening," he prompted.

She hesitated, torn between wanting to tell him how she'd gone from being a mere girl with dreams to a woman who had realized them and wanting to know more about his windsurfer, which had ultimately brought him here. And of course at the same time she realized that neither one was the reason she'd agreed to have dinner with him.

He gave her a patient smile across the table. "We've got ten years to catch up on, Al, minus one night. We're going to be here a while. So talk. Or are you—"

"—chicken?" she finished for him with a knowing smile.

He gave her an unrepentant grin.

"Fine. Here it is in a nutshell."

And she began to talk again. Maybe she could bore him into signing the divorce papers. While they ate, she began the canned account of how she got into her business, the one she hauled out whenever she was interviewed.

But PJ wasn't content with that. He asked questions, drew her out. "Were you scared?" he asked her when she was describing the start-up of her first shop.

"Chicken?" she asked wryly.

"No, really nervous."

She understood the difference. And she nodded. "Felt like I was stepping off into space," she agreed, and recounted the scary times she'd spent on her own, learning what she was capable of, learning what she liked and what she didn't, learning who she was, apart from her father's not-so-dutiful daughter.

It wasn't something she usually did. Ally had learned early that too much reflection meant that she wouldn't get anything done at all. She'd think about things too much, worry about them too much, and so she'd taught herself to weigh her options just long enough to see a clear direction. Then she moved ahead.

She didn't spend a lot of time looking back or analyzing what she'd done. She'd just done it and gone on.

And while she was busy doing, no one was close enough to her or interested enough to ask.

Even when she'd come home, the questions had been few. Her aunt Grace had been impressed. Her father had been too ill to care, and too glad she was home to do more than give thanks that she was there.

Jon thought anything she did was wonderful. He was proud of her. But he was always busy himself. And Ally knew that saving lives was far more important than her "sewing projects" even though he'd never actually said so. He never said much at all about them.

PJ, on the other hand, kept tossing out questions.

And Ally kept answering.

Maybe she answered so expansively because she was proud of what she'd done. Maybe it was to make sure he understood that she had truly taken advantage of the opportunity he'd given her by marrying her, that she'd built something to be proud of, not merely escaped. Maybe it was to show him that she really wasn't the immature rude person she'd been five years ago.

And maybe, she admitted to herself, it was what happened when she found someone interested enough to really listen.

By the time they had finished dinner, she was aware that she had talked more than she'd talked in ages—and PJ had said very little. He sat there, nursing his beer, tipped back in his chair, watching her from beneath hooded lids.

Her awareness of his scrutiny had made Ally keep talking. But finally she stopped and said firmly, "Enough about me. Tell me about you."

It could be opening a Pandora's box.

She might well be better off not knowing anything more about the man who was her husband. But she couldn't not ask. Besides, she really wanted to know.

"You read the newspaper article." He stood up and began to clear the table.

"As you said, blah, blah, blah."

He paused, his hands full of plates. "They got the basics right. More wine?"

Ally shook her head. "No, thanks." She was mellow enough. She needed to move things along. At the back of her mind she could imagine talking to Jon in the morning, facing again the question about whether she'd got things settled.

"So you don't want to talk about what you've been up to?" she pressed. "I thought this was 'catching up' time."

"I work. I play a little softball. When I have a free weekend I go out to Long Island and surf."

"You're living a completely monkish existence, then?"

He grinned. "Doing my best."

Ally rolled her eyes. That certainly wasn't what the article had indicated. But before she could question him further, the doorbell rang.

"Wonder who that could be," PJ murmured as he rinsed the plates and stuck them in the dishwasher.

"Probably your friend Manny from the grocery store, wanting you to make it to the game." Ally stood up, figuring it was time to go anyway.

But PJ shook his head. "He knows better. Sit down," he said. "I'll see who it is. Get rid of them."

She hesitated. But he was already heading toward the front of the apartment.

Ally knew she really should be going. There was no point in staying here any longer. PJ wasn't going to let her use the opportunity to convince him to sign the divorce papers. And as pleasant as it had turned out to be, just sitting around shooting the breeze with him, it was a bad idea.

It was diverting her from her objective. It was making her fall back into the easy familiarity she'd always felt with PJ. Worst of all, it was making her remember the night she'd spent making love with him.

That was past, she reminded herself. Jon was her future.

From the living room she heard voices. PJ's and others'. He wasn't, apparently, "getting rid of them" because as she listened the voices grew closer.

"...don't believe a word of it, for heaven's sake!" a woman's voice said as she came through the doorway and found herself staring straight at Ally.

And Ally found herself staring back at a pixieish woman around thirty with spiky black hair and the most beautifully expressive dark eyes she'd ever seen.

The eyes gaped at her, then flashed accusingly at PJ.

"You mean," the woman demanded, "it's *true?* You really do have a *wife?*"

CHAPTER FOUR

PJ APPEARED in the doorway behind her. "I told you—"

But the woman cut him off. "As if you ever told me the truth." She dismissed him with a briskness that made Ally blink. Then the other woman's hard level gaze swiveled back again to zero in on her. "So," she said, "you're PJ's wife?"

The wealth of doubt and the hard edge of challenge in her voice brought Ally to her feet. They also made her do the one thing she never expected to do.

"Yes," she said, "I am." And she met the woman's gaze with a frank, firm stare of her own. "And who are you?"

Because if this short-haired brunette with her chiseled cheekbones, scarlet lips and tough-girl attitude was one of the women in PJ's life, Ally knew one thing for sure: she was obviously going to have to rescue him from this female's possessive talons before she moved on.

The woman blinked, as if surprised by the question, then drew herself up straight. "I? I'm Cristina."

"My sister, God help me," PJ put in.

"And me," Cristina retorted.

Before Ally could do more than gape, another voice said dryly, "God should really have had mercy on their mother." And a thirtyish man carrying a preschool-aged boy followed PJ and his sister into the room. "Imagine having those two as twins."

Twins?

But even as she heard the word, Ally remembered PJ once remarking that he had a twin. She'd envisioned a cookie-cutter PJ. A less likely looking twin than Cristina was hard to imagine.

PJ's sister was as short as he was tall. Her eyes were brown; his were green. Admittedly they had the same dark hair. But that was the only similarity Ally could see.

"I'm Mark, Cris's husband." The man holding the child offered his hand to Ally with the easy acceptance that his wife completely lacked. "And this is Alex." He jiggled the little boy in his arms. "And your name is...?"

"Ally." Ally shook his hand, smiled at him, winked at Alex who hid his face in his father's shoulder, then peeked at her when he thought she wouldn't notice. He did resemble his uncle, and she had a fleeting sense of what PJ must have looked like as a little boy. Too cute for his own good. She shoved the thought away. "Alice Maruyama...Antonides."

PJ's sister snorted at that. "Where'd you come from?"

"Play nice, Cristina," PJ said gruffly, stepping between them. "Ally came from Hawaii." He gave his sister a hard look that shut her mouth long enough for him to add, "How about some wine? Beer? You're just in time for dessert. We've got pineapple."

"Don't change the subject, PJ." Cristina was still eyeing Ally like an eagle sizing up its prey. "If she's your wife—"

"She is my wife."

"Then I want to know all about her. We didn't believe him when he said he was married," she told Ally as if he weren't standing right there. "We thought he was just trying to avoid all the women Ma and Pa were trying to shove down his throat."

"Cristina—" PJ said sharply.

"I'll take a beer," Mark cut in. "Sit down," he said to his wife while PJ went to the refrigerator to get one. "You're making Ally nervous."

"Good," Cristina said frankly. "If she doesn't have anything to hide she'll be fine."

"What could she have to hide?" Mark looked intrigued.

"Who knows? Where's she been. What's she been doing. Why she's here now." Cristina ticked off plenty of possibilities. All the while studying Ally as if she had her under a microscope. "Maybe she's after his money."

"Well, she certainly isn't after his well-behaved relatives," Mark grinned. "Cristina can be a little, um, protective."

"She thinks I can't fight my own battles," PJ said dryly, coming back to hand his brother-in-law a beer.

"Because I'm older than you," Cristina said loftily.

PJ rolled his eyes. "Four minutes."

"And I'm married—"

"So am I—"

"Which, amazingly, seems to be true. At least, you seem to have produced a wife."

"I didn't produce her. I married her."

"But you don't live with her, either. I, on the other hand, live with my spouse. Always have. And I have a child. So I have a wealth of domestic experience you don't have," she said to her brother with a smug grin. "And I'm looking out for your best interests. So go out in the garden and talk to Mark about his trip. Or baseball. Or boats. And let me do my sisterly duty. Go!" she said again when neither man moved.

Mark looked at PJ. "Your fault."

"I didn't invite her over," PJ protested.

"As if you could have kept her away once she found out Ally was here." Mark laughed and shook his head. "You know what Cristina is like when she's got the bit between her teeth. Might as well let her get on with it."

How had they found out she was here? Ally wondered. But she didn't ask. She just turned to PJ and said stoutly, "Go on. I'm perfectly happy to talk to your sister. I don't need you."

PJ's brows lifted. But Ally met his gaze squarely. And after a long moment he turned to face his sister.

"Do not alienate my wife," he instructed.

Cristina looked indignant. "As if I would!"

"You would," he said with conviction, "if you thought it was a good idea. I'm telling you it's not."

Brother and sister stared at each other. It was like watching mortal combat—death by eye contact.

Clearly his sister brought out a side of PJ that Ally had never seen before. He didn't look particularly upset to have his sister here, but he still looked a little wary—as if he didn't entirely trust her.

Ally wasn't wary or worried. She found herself almost eager to confront PJ's sister. Once she understood who the other woman was, the tension inside her eased. This was no floozy she had to warn off. No woman trying to worm her way into PJ's life.

Warn off? Ally jerked herself up short. What was she thinking? She had no interest in PJ's love life! She was only a wife on paper. His women were nothing to do with her.

Besides, it looked as if Cristina was determined to vet any woman who crossed his path. Ally smiled at the thought, feeling instantly calmer and far more in control.

Also she was curious.

She hadn't expected PJ to tell his family anything about their marriage. Yet apparently he had. So, what had he told them? And when? And why?

She also found herself intrigued by Cristina.

She'd never met any of PJ's family. He had talked about them occasionally. She knew he had grown up in the middle of a boisterous, noisy, demanding Greek-American family.

"I was never alone," he said. "Ever. God, I even had to share the womb. I never had silence. Cristina never shut up. I always had to share a room with my brothers. I never had space."

Ally, who had had far too much loneliness, silence and space in her life, frankly thought PJ's childhood sounded appealing. She'd asked questions, but except for a few comments, whenever he had talked about them it had been mostly about how glad he was they were practically on the other side of the world.

Now, face-to-face with the woman he'd "shared a womb with," Ally couldn't pretend indifference.

Neither apparently could Cristina. The men had barely gone out through the door and slid it shut behind them when PJ's sister sat down at the table opposite Ally and jumped straight in.

If Cristina had ever heard of circumspection or tact, she'd determinedly forgotten everything she'd ever heard. She wanted to know where PJ and Ally had met, when they'd married. And why?

"I wouldn't ask why," she said bluntly, "because ordinarily it would be obvious. You're gorgeous and PJ has always had an eye for a gorgeous woman. But if it were for that reason, he wouldn't have let you walk out of his life again. So…why?"

She regarded Ally intently, and in the face of Cristina's clear concern, Ally found herself answering.

She'd never told anyone else. Besides her father and, recently, Jon, she'd never told a soul she was married.

But this was PJ's sister. Ally didn't have siblings. She had never experienced the bonds that could exist between them. But it was clearly there—and just as much in PJ's words to Cristina as in her attempted defense of him. It bespoke a loyalty and love she could only envy.

And in response, she couldn't deny the kindness he'd done her. Nor could she minimize it or pretend it had been some frivolous or foolish thing they had done.

And so she began to talk.

She spoke haltingly at first about her father's demands on her—about what she should take in university, about what job she would hold when she finished, about the man he expected her to marry. It sounded medieval and melodramatic to her ears as she told it, and she fully expected Cristina would roll her eyes.

Instead the other woman listened raptly and nodded more and more vigorously.

"Fathers!" she muttered, eyes flashing in indignation. "Mine is just as bad. They always think they know what's best. And they can be so clueless!"

But her indignation vanished and she beamed gleefully when Ally told her about her grandmother's legacy and how she could use it to avoid having to fall in with her father's demands.

"I couldn't be the person he wanted me to be. I needed to be me. To get away and find out who I was. But I couldn't get away without the legacy. And I couldn't have the legacy without being married—"

"So PJ married you!" Cristina clapped her hands together delightedly, her eyes were alight with satisfaction. And all her original skepticism and animosity toward Ally seemed to evaporate.

"That is such a great story." She cheered Ally's determination—and her brother's part in it. "I should have known he wouldn't do anything stupid."

She didn't even blame Ally for "using" him to get what she needed.

"Blame you?" she'd said, affronted, when Ally suggested it. "Of course not! What else could you have done?"

Ally shook her head, surprised at Cristina's approbation.

"So what did you do? Where did you go?" PJ's sister asked.

And Ally told her that as well. And in telling her the truth about how she had used PJ to get her legacy, to get her education, to travel and learn and work and become the person she'd become, far from putting Cristina off, actually brought her around to Ally's side.

"I think it's absolutely marvelous. What a hero!" And for an instant Ally thought Cristina might jump up and go outside and throw her arms around her brother. Instead she just shook her head and aimed a smile and a fond glance his way.

Ally, following her gaze, knew that what Cristina said was true. "He was, actually," she admitted quietly as much to herself as to his sister.

"And of course you couldn't stay. You had to leave," Cristina went on, telling the story herself now, and believing every word she said. "To find yourself. And PJ was probably distraught, but knew he had to let you go."

"I don't think he was distraught," Ally said.

"Of course he was. How could he not be? You're everything he'd want in a woman." Cristina looked her over with frank admiration. "He's not blind."

Ally felt her cheeks warm. "It wasn't quite like that. Besides, he wasn't ready to be married then. Not *really* married."

"You mean, adult and responsible and all? Yes, I can see that." Cristina's tone grew thoughtful, as if she were remembering, too, what he'd been like ten years ago. "He was a kid. I remember what he was like when he left—moody, distant, could hardly wait to be on his own. Independent to a fault. Yes, he would have needed time and space to find himself, too. But now—" Cristina's voice brightened visibly "—he has. You both have."

"Yes." Ally nodded, glad PJ's sister understood. Now she could explain about why she'd come, why it was time for them to go their separate ways.

"And so you've come back to him." Cristina sighed in pure appreciation. She smiled broadly. "That is soooo romantic. Who'd ever think PJ would be romantic?"

"He's not!" Ally blurted, and this time, at least, she managed to get the words out before Cristina could cut her off.

Cristina looked startled at her vehemence. But then she laughed and gestured toward the living room. "Maybe not. But if he's not a romantic, why did he have Martha paint that mural?"

Ally stared, uncomprehending.

Cristina shook her head. "We didn't understand what he was up to. But it makes sense now." She glanced back toward the living room and its resident mural. "Trust me, under all that cool, PJ's a romantic. And so are you."

There was only one time in her life Ally thought she'd behaved romantically—and that had been the night she'd spent in PJ's arms.

Before and after, she'd been a realist. She'd done what she

needed to do. She was still doing it. She was being a realist now, asking for the divorce, not asking for the impossible.

She was being a realist in choosing to marry Jon, who wanted the same things she did, who felt about her the way she felt about him. She was, she realized, the daughter her father had wanted her to be, after all.

"I'm not a romantic, either," she told Cristina.

But PJ's sister disagreed. Her eyes widened. Her hands fluttered. "Just turning up on his doorstep isn't romantic?" She laughed and shook her head. "It's the most romantic thing I can imagine."

"I didn't mean—"

But Cristina leaned toward Ally across the table and lowered her voice, as if the men outside might be able to overhear. "I know. You don't want to scare him to death. Men can be panicky that way. But, honestly, you picked the perfect time. No matter what he thinks. PJ is ready to be married now. He's settled. Centered. And he dotes on the kids. You should see him with the nephews."

In fact Ally could see PJ with Alex right now.

Other than when he'd tossed a ball or a Frisbee to a kid on the beach, it was the first time she'd seen him interacting with a child. She'd imagined he might be awkward. Lots of men were.

For that matter, she was. She'd simply had no experience with them. But PJ had apparently had plenty. Or dealing with them came naturally to him.

Ally had expected to see Alex cling to his father and duck his head when PJ talked to him, just as the little boy had with her. But the minute they'd gone outside, Alex had flung himself into his uncle's arms. And PJ had accepted him willingly, flipping him up and over his shoulders, then whipping him around his side and tossing the boy into the air.

Ally had watched in almost horrified amazement. But PJ seemed perfectly comfortable, and Alex, shrieking with laughter, clearly loved it.

After that PJ had hung Alex upside down, let the boy climb his legs like a logger going up a ponderosa pine, then somersault to the ground. He was like a human climbing frame and Alex was having the time of his life. Even when they stopped, Alex remained sitting on his shoulders while PJ stood there, listening to Mark.

"PJ will be a great dad." Cristina stated the obvious. "Are you going to have kids soon?"

Ally colored fiercely. "No! I mean—we're not...!"

"Sorry," Cristina said quickly. "That really is none of my business. It's enough that you're back. Whatever happens, happens, right?"

"Y-yes," Ally managed. She needed to say it—to tell this woman why she'd really come. But somehow the words wouldn't form. Because they shouldn't come from her, Ally told herself. They should come from PJ. He was the one who had told his sister he was married. He needed to be the one to tell her they were getting a divorce.

And when he had kids someday—when he was some child's wonderful father—that child would not be hers. And if the thought caused pain, Ally didn't let herself think about it.

"Mom and Dad will be so pleased," Cristina went on. "Mom can hardly wait to meet you."

"What?" Ally's brain jerked back to the moment. "Oh, no!"

Cristina made a face. "You aren't going to be able to keep her away. She was so excited to hear you'd finally turned up. She said she'd always believed PJ—about being married. Dad thought he was stonewalling. Dad thought he might have even faked the marriage certificate. But Ma said no. So did *Yiayia*—our grandmother. *Yiayia* said he wouldn't lie about a thing like that."

He'd told them all? He actually showed them their marriage certificate? Ally's brain spun.

Cristina didn't notice. She shook her head. "She was right. Mother's intuition, you think? Before I had Alex, I'd have laughed at that. Now sometimes I think I know what he'll do before he does it. So she may be right."

"No, she's not right!"

At Ally's outburst, Cristina's eyes fastened on her. "What do you mean? You said you were married."

"We are." She chewed on her lip briefly, torn. What could she say? Talk about opening a can of worms. "For the moment," she said at last.

Cristina's gaze snapped up and she frowned. Then her expression lightened. "Oh, are you worried that you might not suit now, after all this time? Don't be. You're soul mates, it will work out."

Ally opened her mouth to deny it, but again the words wouldn't come out. And she couldn't tell Cristina about coming here to get him to sign divorce papers. If he'd kept their marriage a secret, it wouldn't really have mattered. Everyone would know he didn't care. But he'd told them he was married to her.

Word of the divorce would have to be his to tell.

Cristina patted her hand. "Don't worry. It will be fine. The only one who's going to be upset is Dad."

"What does your father have to do with it?" Just what she needed. One more person's opinion to matter.

"Oh, he's a 'never say die' sort. He's still trying to hook PJ up with Connie Cristopolous. Her whole family is coming from Greece this weekend. It's a huge affair. Sort of a family reunion for us, too. Complete with fatted calf or, in this case, sacrificial lamb. At least, it was. That was going to be PJ." Cristina laughed. "But not now, obviously. With a wife in tow, he won't have to worry."

"But I'm not—"

"Poor Dad," Cristina said with relish. "Well, it serves him right. He should have believed." She shrugged. "It doesn't matter. It might be a little awkward at first, but he'll be thrilled to have a son married off and no wedding to have to go to. Dad much prefers sailing and golf."

Before Ally could even begin to think of how to respond to that, Mark opened the sliding door.

"Someone needs to go home to bed," he said. Alex was back in his arms, head against his father's shoulder, looking weepy and out of sorts.

"Yes. And we should let these two enjoy each other's company." Cristina smiled warmly at Ally and then at PJ who, seeing the smile, raised his brows quizzically.

Cristina stood up and went over to him, going up on her toes to kiss his cheek. "I like your wife," she said. "A lot."

The vehemence of her declaration seemed to surprise him. But then he just looked bemused. "She checks out okay, then?"

Cristina swatted his arm. "You knew she would. You married her. You are such a dark horse."

"Me?"

"Such a romantic. Riding in to save her like a knight on a charger."

PJ reddened. "I never—"

"A knight? PJ?" Mark's brows rose. He regarded his brother-in-law with wonder.

"A knight," Cristina said firmly. "Who'd a thunk it? Come on. Let's go home." She linked her arm in Mark's. "And I'll tell you all about it."

At the door, she turned back and looked at Ally. "I want to hear more about your art. And the clothes. They sound fantastic. We didn't even get into that," she said to her brother. "But we will. There's plenty of time now." She went out, then turned to back Ally. "You can fill me in on the weekend."

"The weekend?" Ally stared.

"Oh, I know everyone else will want a piece of you, too. But we're going to talk."

"I'm not—"

"Are you going up Friday?" Cristina asked her brother.

"Yes."

"No!" Ally blurted.

"We're still discussing it," PJ said smoothly.

Cristina laughed and patted his cheek. "Enjoy the discussion.

And the making up after." She winked. "We'll be there Saturday. See you then."

"Yes," PJ said.

"No!" Ally said.

"Oh, this is going to be fun," Cristina said happily. Then as PJ began to close the door, impulsively his sister darted back in to plant a quick kiss on Ally's cheek.

Her eyes were shining and she squeezed Ally's hand as she said, "I just want to say how happy I am for both of you. And...welcome to the family."

CHAPTER FIVE

"No!" THE door had barely shut behind Cristina and Mark before Ally had the word out of her mouth. "I am *not* going to your parents' house."

"Al—"

"No!" She whirled away from where she'd been standing beside him near the door, stalking across the room, needing to put as much space between them as possible.

Only when she was as far as she could get did she turn and glare at him. "You did this on purpose!"

"Did what?" How could he look so innocent? So completely guileless.

"You set me up! You invited your sister here so she would jump to all the wrong conclusions and then back me into a corner where you think I'll be forced to go to your parents' house with you! Well, I won't!"

"I didn't invite my sister here."

Ally snorted. "Then how did she know to come? She knew I was here."

"They invited me for dinner tonight. I had to decline."

"And you just happened to mention—"

"I didn't even talk to her. I asked Rosie to call her."

"And Rosie just happened to mention—"

He shrugged. "If she did, you can blame yourself as much as me. Who came in and announced she was my wife?"

Ally's teeth came together with a snap. "In my office we prize confidentiality."

"In mine we prize people," he said mildly, putting her back up even further. At the same time she knew he was right. She'd told his assistant who she was. She'd used the relationship first.

"Besides, it doesn't make any difference. You weren't a complete surprise. They knew about you."

Ally couldn't even imagine how that conversation must have gone. "So it seems. And what did you say, 'Oh, by the way, I'm married, but I seem to have mislaid my wife'?"

His lips pressed into a thin line. "The first part, yes. The second didn't come into it. It just…happened. When I came back and decided to stick around, Dad and Mom started throwing women my way. I said I wasn't interested. They said, 'Oh, God, he's gay.'" His mouth twisted. "I suppose I could have let them think that, but it seemed smarter to tell them the truth. So I said, 'No, I'm married.'"

"And they didn't say, 'Show us your wife'?"

"Of course they did. But I couldn't, could I?"

"So what did you do?"

"Told them a shortened version of what happened. Said I'd met you in Hawaii. That we were friends. That you needed to get married. That I married you."

"You said I *needed* to get married? Oh, for God's sake, do they think I was *pregnant?*"

"It did occur to my mother," he admitted. "She asked, rather hopefully, as I recall, if she was going to have another grandchild. Cristina had just had Alex. I said no. I said you needed to stop your father meddling in your life, and marrying me was how you'd done it. No big deal."

Ally's eyes widened. "And they were okay with that?"

"Well, it wasn't their idea of a best-case scenario. They like their children to marry people they can meet and who will have loads of little Antonides babies." He gave her a wry smile and a shrug. "That's the way they are. But what were they going to say?"

Ally couldn't imagine. She knew what her father would have said. It wouldn't have been pretty. She shook her head. She prowled restlessly around PJ's living room, feeling off balanced. Awkward. Guilty.

She'd never really considered how their whole marriage scene would play out for PJ. It had always been about her. Her needs. Her hopes.

"Of course they wanted to meet you," PJ went on. "They wanted to know where you were. What you were doing. When we were going to get back together."

Ally cocked her head. "And you said…?"

"I said I didn't know." He lifted his shoulders, spread his hands. "I didn't, did I? The truth."

Ally grimaced. The truth was supposed to set you free, wasn't it? She didn't feel free at all. She felt trapped, hemmed in.

She picked up the softball on the bookcase and slapped it against her palm. "And now Cristina assumes I'm going to the family reunion with you."

"It's a natural assumption."

"And what will they think when we get a divorce? They'll have expectations," Ally went on. "Cristina certainly has expectations!"

"She likes you." He still sounded almost surprised at that.

Unaccountably, the thought made Ally bristle. "You thought she wouldn't?"

"Nothing Cristina does surprises me. But I didn't know if she'd shut up long enough to find out anything about you. Cristina generally goes into every situation with both guns firing. My sister shoots first and asks questions later. I figured she would like you a lot if she gave you a chance. And apparently she did." He paused. "What did you tell her?"

"The truth."

"That you came for a divorce?" The edge was back in his voice, but he looked perplexed as he said it. "But she didn't—"

"I told her the truth about why we got married. About my meddling father. About needing to find myself. About not marrying Ken. About the legacy. I told her why you married me. She thinks you're a hero."

A grin lit PJ's face. "She said that? I wish you'd got it on tape. It won't happen again in my lifetime."

"She's very devoted. And far fonder of you than you might imagine. She was definitely protective."

"Bossy," PJ corrected.

"She loves you." Ally envied him that familial closeness. She'd never had it. "What you did—she thinks it's the most romantic thing she's ever heard."

PJ laughed. "You put a spell on her!"

"No. She put one on herself. I told her the truth—and she embroidered it to fit her view of the world."

"That's pretty much Cristina in a nutshell. Still, you apparently handled her very well."

"If I had, she wouldn't have assumed I was staying."

"Why didn't you tell her that you weren't?"

"I thought it was your place to do that."

"Mine?"

"Because you said we were married. I felt you should be the one to tell them we're getting a divorce."

"I'm not. You are."

And they were back to that again, damn it. "All right, fine. That *I'm* getting a divorce! Anyway, I didn't think you'd appreciate me announcing first thing that *I'd* come to get a divorce. And Cristina didn't ask why I was there. She just assumed…and then she assumed some more. And more. And finally she just leaped to the conclusion that I'd be coming with you on the weekend."

"Imagine that," PJ murmured.

"You could have told her I wasn't!"

"But I want you to come."

"What?" She stared at him. "Oh, come on, PJ."

"Why not? It's a family reunion among other things. You're family."

"I am not!"

"Legally, you are. And of course you should come. Let my folks meet you. See that you're real. That I didn't make you up." He grinned.

"Raise their expectations," Ally muttered.

The grin widened. "Save me from the clutches of Connie Cristopolous."

"Oh, please." She rolled her eyes. "You can save yourself."

"I did you a favor once."

The words dropped quietly between them. An observation. A statement of fact. A reproach. All of the above.

Ally wanted to rake her hands through her hair. Her fingers tightened on the ball, as if she would squeeze it to death.

PJ didn't say a word, just stood there, watched her. Looked expectant.

Ally ground her teeth. "Damn you. I never should have come. I should have mailed you the damn papers." She spun away and paced around the room, furious at having been trapped, knowing she had no choice.

She sighed and tried one last time. "It's a bad idea. Going out to your folks' place will just make things worse."

"For who?"

"For you! If I show up with you, they'll expect us to be a couple after that. And they'll be appalled when you tell them we're getting a divorce."

He propped an arm on the mantel of the fireplace. "Why would I tell them that?"

"Because we are! I am!" she said before he could correct her pronoun.

"But I don't want a divorce."

"Damn it!" She wanted to wring his neck. "Why not? And don't tell me you're so afraid of Connie Cristopolous that you want to stay married so your parents don't try shoving her down your throat."

"Well, it is a consideration."

"I'm sure it is," Ally said bitterly. "You're just trying to be difficult."

He gave her a lopsided grin. "Not really."

"Yes, you are! I shouldn't have come here. Not to New York. Not to dinner! And now I need to leave." She grabbed her purse off the bookcase and headed for the door.

PJ stepped in front of it. "Don't be in such a hurry."

"What point is there in staying? We're not getting anywhere."

"We might be."

Her gaze narrowed. "What's that supposed to mean?"

"We're getting to know each other again."

"Just what we want," Ally said acerbically. "PJ, enough! I realize I've handled things badly. I know I should have got the divorce out of the way before I ever let things go so far with Jon. But I had no idea where you were. And I didn't realize things were going so fast. My dad's illness just sort of…accelerated things, and it just seemed like it was meant to be— between Jon and me."

"Jon and me. Jon and me." His tone was mocking. "If he's your dear true love, where is he? Why didn't he come with you?"

"Because he's busy. He's a doctor, for heaven's sake! He doesn't have time to run around chasing down my soon-to-be-ex-husband."

"Does he have time for you?"

"Of course he does! He takes time when I'm there. I give him a reason to take time," she said. And that was the truth. Without her Jon was consumed only by his work. "He loves me. I love him. And we want to get married, have a family, give my dad a grandchild. He wants a chance to meet his grandchild. And his health is poor. Time is of the essence."

"So stick with me. We're further down the road."

"What?" She stared at him.

He spread his hands. "We're already married. We wouldn't have to waste time. No waiting for a divorce. We could have a family," PJ said. "Give him a grandchild. What do you say?"

She wanted to scream.

And worse—in some tiny deranged part of her brain—she wanted to say, *Yes!*

Because Ally knew that if PJ had said those words ten years ago, after one night in his arms, no matter that they had planned it to be purely a marriage of convenience, she would have flung good sense and caution to the winds and believed they could make a marriage work.

Because right then—on that one night—PJ had touched her with such a mixture of passion and reverence, eagerness and gentleness that she'd actually dared to think he might really love her.

But *this* PJ?

This PJ was toying with her.

Oh, she had no doubt he was perversely serious about wanting her to come to his parents' place. It would doubtless suit him to make sure his father and Connie Whosits knew he really was married.

In fact, he might simply want to stay married to her as a way of avoiding all future entanglements.

But there was no love involved.

As for wanting a child, well, maybe he did. Cristina seemed to think he was ready to settle down and have children. And of course, to his mind she would be convenient for that, too.

"I have half a mind to come with you," she snapped. "Then go back home to Hawaii and leave you to sort things out. It would serve you right. Your mother knows I'm here. Did you know that?"

PJ shook his head. "No. But I can't say I'm surprised. Cristina never could keep a secret."

"Did you expect her to?"

"Not really."

It was the last straw. He'd planned this whole thing, had been manipulating her all evening.

He'd set her up to deal with Cristina, had known his sister would pressure her into coming. He'd fully expected his sister to tell his mother. She supposed she was lucky that Mrs. Antonides hadn't turned up on the doorstep, as well.

Well, be careful what you wish for, buster, she thought grimly.

"Fine. I'll do it! You want me to meet your parents, I'll come with you and meet your parents. I'll be your wife for the weekend. I'll be sweet and charming and wonderful. But after that you are on your own. The scales are balanced. You did me a favor. I'm doing you one. We'll be even. And then, damn it, PJ Antonides, I'm filing for divorce!"

That went well, PJ thought grimly with more than a little self-mockery.

He stood outside the hotel in midtown Manhattan where he'd just left Ally and stuffed his hands in his pockets, shaking his head.

She'd insisted on leaving once she'd agreed to come to his parents' on Friday. He'd invited her to stay at his place.

"Why not? We might as well begin as we mean to go on," he'd said.

And Ally's black eyes had flashed. "We don't mean to go on. At least I don't. One weekend, PJ. That's all."

And he might not have seen Ally for ten years, but he knew her limits. And the look on her face said that he'd pushed her far enough. He'd shrugged.

"I'll see you back to your hotel."

She'd argued about that. But he wasn't taking no for an answer when it came to seeing her safely back to her room. She might have taken care of herself for ten years, but it was his turn now. At least for tonight. So they'd taken a cab across the river to the big midtown Manhattan hotel where she was staying.

She'd thanked him politely for "the lovely evening" as the cab had drawn up outside the main entrance. He knew she didn't mean it. He also knew she'd mean it less by the time he really said good-night.

"Put your money away," he'd said sharply. "And don't say good-night yet. I'm not leaving."

He'd followed her out of the taxi, paid the driver, then hurried to catch up with her as she was already inside the lobby. It was all polished marble and crystal chandeliers.

"This is totally unnecessary," Ally insisted. "You can go home now. You never felt compelled to see me to my door before."

"That was then. This is now. That was Hawaii. This is New York City. Humor me."

She just looked at him and shook her head. But when he persisted, she shrugged. "Suit yourself." And she turned and marched to the elevator. "But don't expect me to invite you in."

He didn't expect she would.

If there was one thing he'd learned from his years on the beach, it was how to bide his time. You couldn't rush the ocean. When you went out on the water, surfing or windsurfing, success didn't come from pushing or trying to control.

You got into position and you watched and you waited. You learned patience and awareness. And timing.

When the time was right—when you and the wave were in sync—then and only then did you move.

And just like he couldn't push a wave, PJ knew he couldn't push Ally Maruyama.

So he simply accompanied her up in the elevator and down the corridor to her room. He waited silently until she opened the door of her room. He didn't press. Didn't invite himself in or suggest that she should.

"I'll see you Friday at noon," he said. "I'll pick you up."

"I still think this is insane, PJ. How are you going to explain later to your family? You don't know what you're asking."

PJ knew exactly what he was asking. But he didn't think she did. "If you get bored tomorrow, call me."

"I won't be bored," Ally said. "I have an appointment with a gallery owner."

He paused. "Who?"

"Gabriela del Castillo. She's shown some of my work at her gallery in Santa Fe."

PJ knew the name. His sister Martha had mentioned her. Said glowing things. "She going to show your stuff here?"

"I'll know more tomorrow. Thank you again for dinner," she said, once more sounding like the proper well-brought-up girl he remembered. "And for the introduction to your sister," she added a bit grimly.

He grinned. "My pleasure."

"Good night."

"Good night," he said equally politely. But then as she started to close the door, he stopped her. "Ally."

She narrowed her gaze. "What? I told you I'm not inviting you in, PJ. I've got work to do, Jon to call, things to think about. What do you want?"

"Just—" he hesitated, but only for a split second "—this."

And he took one step forward, swept his arms around her, hauled her close and set his lips on hers.

It wasn't planned. PJ didn't plan.

He was an "act now, revise later" sort of guy. He believed in a spur-of-the-moment, caution-be-damned, full-speed-ahead approach to life. Always had. Probably always would.

It had got him into some scrapes. It had got him into a marriage. It had got him where he was today—kissing Ally.

Dear God, yes, he was kissing Ally.

The quick peck he'd managed when she'd come out of the subway had barely given him a taste. But it had whetted his appetite, made him remember the last time he'd kissed Ally.

For ten years he'd wanted more.

And now he had it. Had her lips under his, warm and soft. Resisting at first, pressed together, unyielding. He touched them with his tongue, teased them, and rejoiced when they parted to draw a breath.

It came as a gasp almost. "P—"

But he didn't let her speak. Didn't want to hear what she'd say. So he pressed his advantage, moved in, took more.

And the more he took, the more he wanted. The more the

memories crowded in, the more the woman in his arms seemed to melt against him. His body hardened in response. His heart pounded.

He wanted—! He needed—!

And he knew she did, too. He could feel her softening against him, could feel her whole body now, pressed against his, molding itself to his. Oh, yes! He deepened the kiss.

And the instant that he did, she jerked out of his embrace, pulled back, her eyes wide, her cheeks flushed, mouth a perfect O. He could see the pulse hammer at her throat. She gripped the door so tightly her knuckles were white.

"That," she said icily, "was totally unnecessary."

Slowly PJ shook his head. "Was it?" he said, his own heart hammering so hard he could barely talk. "I don't think so." He managed a lopsided grin. "Tell that to Jon when you talk to him."

And he turned and walked away.

His body would much rather have been doing something else.

"The message you left on my machine was garbled," Jon said. "It sounded like you said you were staying longer."

Ally, who had grabbed her mobile phone when it rang, even though she was still asleep, barely made sense of what he was saying. She pushed herself up in bed and squinted at the clock—9:30 a.m.?

She never slept that late!

But then, as a rule, she didn't lie awake half the night wondering if she'd lost her mind, either.

Last night clearly she had.

She'd shut the door on PJ, bolted it, then leaned against it, breathing as hard as if she'd run a marathon. A marathon would have made more sense!

She would have prepared herself, she would have trained for a marathon.

She hadn't been prepared for PJ. Or for his refusal to sign

the divorce papers. Or for his sister. Or for her agreement to go
to his parents' for the weekend.

Or most especially for his kiss.

Dear God, that kiss.

She'd just been congratulating herself on having made it back
to her room, if not emotionally totally intact, at least unscathed.

And then he'd kissed her. And ten years of carefully papered-
over need had come spilling out of her. Ten years of memories
locked down and shut away had swamped her, and she had been
powerless against the force of them.

Of course, she'd had only a split second's warning.

She had seen something in his eyes at that last second when
she'd started to close the door, something that looked hard and
dangerous and tempting. But she'd discounted it. Had thought
she was safe. Home free.

Wrong.

Very *very* wrong.

Every time she'd closed her eyes all night long, she'd been
swept back to that kiss. The way his mouth had awakened her,
the way the press of his body had made her feel. She'd felt
branded, possessed. And unthinking, she'd responded with a
hunger of her own. It was a feeling she'd only experienced once
before in her life. That night...

Their wedding night.

She had relived it all—that night and this for hours. It was no
wonder she hadn't slept much. It was a wonder she'd slept at all.

"Did you say that or was I hearing things?" Jon said, jerking
her back to something else she wasn't prepared for.

She had called him last night as she'd promised. She'd
waited until she thought she could put together a coherent
sentence or two, had hoped Jon would be there to say sensible
things, to remind her about her father, about her life in
Honolulu, and the world beyond PJ's kiss.

But she'd only got his answering machine, so she'd left a

message. Now she said, "Um, yes. That's what I said. You got it right."

She sat up straighter in the bed, pushed herself back against the headboard and willed herself to sound brisk and in control—not to mention "awake"—though God knew she wasn't at all. She hadn't fallen asleep until dawn. "I'm staying over the weekend," she said.

"What about the hospital benefit on Saturday? You didn't forget."

She had actually. But she also remembered something else. "You said you couldn't go to the benefit," she reminded him. "When I was planning the trip I asked you about it, and you said it wasn't a problem, that you couldn't go, you were too busy."

"I am busy. But I need to go. Fogarty says I'm expected to show my face."

Fogarty was the head honcho in Jon's practice, the senior doctor whose lead everyone else followed. "Then I guess you'll have to show your face. But you'll have to do it alone because I can't be there."

"Ally, what's going on?"

"Something's come up. Something important."

"What could possibly be more important? The benefit is important, Alice."

But it hadn't been until Fogarty had decided it was. "I know. And I did ask," she said again. "But I've made a commitment here now. I have some…unfinished business."

"I know you want that Castillo woman to take you on, but really, Ally, you have plenty of exposure elsewhere. And when we're married, how are you going to keep all the shops supplied? When we have kids…?"

They'd had this discussion before. And after they had children, Ally was certainly willing to put her career on hold and be a full-time mother. She had made up her mind some time ago that if she were ever fortunate enough to have children, she didn't want someone else to raise them. If it were an economic necessity, she would certainly work to support them. But it wasn't. Jon could provide the economic security for the family while the children were young.

Until then, however, she wanted to work, to draw, to paint, to design, to sew.

"When we have kids, I will put them first," she said firmly. "But now I have to stay here until Monday."

And she wasn't entirely averse to taking advantage of the fact that he had assumed it had to do with her art. After all, if she told him why she was really staying, he would like it even less.

"Your dad is going to be disappointed. He was looking forward to seeing you tomorrow."

"I know." Ally felt guilty, but she didn't see any other option. "Well, I'll see him Monday. And if you stop in to see him today, give him my love."

"I doubt if I'll have time to stop by. I have a full day."

"I'll give him a ring, then," Ally said. "And I'll call you as soon as I know what flight on Monday I'll get in on."

"Right. I'll try to be there to pick you up. But I have to go now. I have surgery in less than an hour."

"Right. Of course. Thanks for calling back. And I really am sorry about the weekend. I'll talk to you later. Love you."

But Jon had already hung up.

Ally sat there holding the phone in her hand, feeling sick.

She knew she was letting him down. She knew he counted on her. Depended on her. Loved her. And she knew he didn't understand about PJ. Probably he never would. She wished she'd been able to talk to him. It would have helped so much to have felt able to confide in him about what had happened, to admit that PJ's refusal to sign the papers had unnerved her, that the meal he'd cooked had baffled her, that his sister had charmed her, that going to meet his parents was seriously rattling her.

And then there was his kiss.

Her senses still spun, her brain still whirled every time she thought about that kiss. But of course Jon was the last person she could talk to about any of that.

Would PJ kiss her again this weekend?

Did she want him to?

If he did, how would she react a second time? Why was he doing it? What did he want? He didn't love her.

Did she still, somewhere deep inside, love him?

And if she did, what then?

CHAPTER SIX

EVERYONE in the office knew about Ally's arrival.

PJ knew Rosie had told his sister. Hell, he'd *wanted* her to tell Cristina. But had she had to tell everyone?

Not that anyone said anything. It was in the way they looked at him and in what they didn't say that told him they all knew.

The minute he'd opened the office door Thursday morning, the conversation had stopped. Rosie and the rest of them had been in deep discussion, and at the sight of him, the room went from full babble to total silence.

They all turned and stared. No one said a word.

"High-level top-secret meeting?" he asked blandly. "Or are you all speechless in admiration of my tie?" He flapped his silver-and-black-striped tie at them and raised a sardonic brow.

One of the architects grinned, flashing his gold tooth, then shook his dreads and headed for his office. "Sorry, boss. Not my style."

The others turned red and mumbled something before vanishing, as well, leaving only Rosie to meet his hard stare unflinchingly.

"Did you put out a bulletin?" he asked acidly.

"Mark was already here this morning," she said. No further explanation was needed.

"Ah. Sorry." He grimaced and headed for his office. He hadn't slept most of the night. He'd prowled and paced and remembered. Lay down. Got up. Relived. And this morning he was edgy and he knew it.

"Ryne Murray will be here at nine," Rosie said to his back.

"Let me know when he gets here." He spoke without turning around, happy to close the door behind him before Rosie could decide that, even though it was business as usual, she was still entitled to ask questions.

He wouldn't mind the questions, PJ thought, tossing his jacket over the back of his chair, then going to stare out the window, provided he knew the answers.

But whatever she might ask about Ally—and he knew that all of Rosie's questions would deal with Ally—PJ didn't have any answers at all.

No, not true.

He had one: he still wanted her.

When he'd married her, PJ had expected nothing. And that was pretty much exactly what he'd got.

After the ceremony—if you could even call it that—where they'd said their vows at the courthouse, when they'd come back outside into the bright Honolulu sunlight, he'd suggested a celebratory dinner.

"After all," he'd told her, grinning, "it's not every day we get married."

But the smile Ally returned had been tremulous at best. "I don't think so. I just—well, I really need to tell my father I'm married."

As that had been the point of the whole exercise, PJ hadn't argued. "Okay. I'll come with you. Moral support."

He'd thought she'd jump at the chance. But she'd declined that, too, shaking her head and saying gravely, "Thanks, but you'd better not. I don't think it would be a good idea. This is between him and me. It wouldn't be fair to bring you into it."

He was already in it. He'd married her, hadn't he? How much more "in it" could he get? But he knew that hadn't even occurred to her. He wasn't sure that it ever would.

But he hadn't argued. He'd married her for her sake.

To his way of thinking she deserved the same freedom to find herself that he'd got by moving away from his family. The fact that he didn't have to marry anyone to achieve it was lucky for him. If she didn't want it to be his business, well then, it wouldn't be his business, he'd decided.

It wasn't as if this was some love match. It was just the sort of thing one spur-of-the-moment impulsive friend would do for another.

"Okay. Suit yourself," he'd said.

But for a long moment neither had moved. Their gazes had locked, and perhaps a faint notion of what they'd just done inside the courthouse occurred to Ally then.

If it had, though, she thrust it away, saying, "I probably won't see you again. I'll be leaving in the morning."

He'd nodded. "Yeah, sure." Then he'd cracked a grin. "Well, good luck. Have a good life."

She'd smiled, too. And they'd both laughed a little awkwardly. She'd said something about he should feel free to get a divorce whenever. And then she'd stuck out her hand to say farewell.

He could still remember that. She'd married him—then shaken his hand. He remembered her touch. Her grasp had been soft and gentle. Just the slightest pressure. Her palm was cold and clammy even though the temperature had been hot that day. He'd wanted to warm it as he'd squeezed her fingers in his big rough callused hand.

He'd wanted to warm *her.* And so as soon as she moved to ease her fingers out of his grasp, he let them go, only to reach out an instant later and wrap his arms around her, draw her slender body against his and touched his lips to hers.

It wasn't intended to be a moment of erotic passion.

It was supposed to comfort, encourage, sustain. And yet, the taste of her, the feel of her soft lips under the hard pressure of his awoke something wholly unintended.

"Warm" didn't even begin to cover what he had felt. And

which of them was more shaken when at last he broke it off, he could not have said.

Ally had stared at him, her eyes wide and astonished. She looked stunned, which was no more than he felt.

And then she said, "I have to go," and turned and ran down the sidewalk as if all the demons in hell were after her.

And PJ had stood there wondering what had hit him.

He had still been wondering when he'd gone to bed that night—his wedding night.

The very notion seemed like some sort of perverse joke. He'd avoided going home for hours. He had gone surfing at dusk, then out drinking with a couple of buddies, doing his best to put it out of his mind.

But he'd still been thinking about it—about *her*—when he'd heard a light knock on the door.

His landlady, Mrs. Chang, was usually in bed before now. But sometimes she came to get him when she needed something on a high shelf or wanted him to open the lid on a jar.

He wasn't much in the mood for Mrs. Chang tonight. He'd been "useful" already once today: he'd married Ally.

But when the knocking continued and grew even more persistent, he got up and opened the door, then stood stock-still and stared at Ally standing there looking at him with wide unreadable eyes.

"What's wrong? Did your old man—"

She swallowed again and gave her head a little shake. "No. I just thought that, um, it's our wedding night and—could you make love with me?"

You could have knocked him over with a breath. He stared at her in astonishment, knowing he should ask her to repeat it, but not wanting to have his dearest dream snatched away when she repeated whatever it was she'd actually said.

But then she went on, "I just…it's a marriage, PJ—and I don't know, it doesn't seem like a marriage. But I thought it might if…I just want it to be real."

A slow smile had dawned. He'd shaken his head, dazed and delighted, astonished at the strange turns of fate, and not about to question his good luck.

"It will be my pleasure," he'd assured her.

And his responsibility. Loving Ally was no problem at all. Being responsible for making her first time—and he was sure it was her first time—good was something else. He was young. Eager. Not untried, of course. But definitely not the most skilled of lovers.

But this was Ally, and she was depending on him. She was trusting him. And he was determined to love her the way she deserved.

He did ask, "Are you sure, Al? Are you sure this is what you want?" because he didn't want there to be any misunderstanding.

She'd nodded jerkily, gulping again, looking terrified. "It is," she insisted. Then, at his look of skepticism, she'd said it again. "I mean it, PJ. I want to."

And then, as if she were determined to convince him, she'd put her hands on his bare chest and leaned in to press a tentative kiss against his lips.

And he'd been lost.

PJ had made love with a few women in his life. It was enjoyable tactile exercise—and nothing felt better. But he learned very quickly that making love with Ally went far beyond that. It wasn't just exercise. It didn't just feel good.

It felt right.

As he unbuttoned her shirt, he found his own fingers trembling. And when he pressed kisses along her jawline and licked the edge of her ear, her tiny gasps sent his heart into overdrive. He almost couldn't get her shirt off. They might have been tangled in it forever if she hadn't finished unfastening the buttons and skimmed it away, then pressed closer to him.

Her skin was petal soft. And warm. Not cold and clammy as her hand had been when she'd offered it outside the courthouse. Now her skin was hot satin beneath his fingers. He stroked and kissed, nibbled and laved. Her small breasts were perfect in the scrap of rose-colored lace that was her bra. But they were even more enticing when he freed them.

And when she arched beneath the touch of his lips on first one nipple and then the other, his own desire almost betrayed him right there.

He backed off, pulled away to take deep harsh breaths, to regain control. He dropped his head so that his hair brushed against her breasts, so that his mouth was barely more than an inch from her navel.

He felt her fingers in his hair, gripping, tugging. "What?" he muttered.

"Y-you're breathing."

An anguished laugh made it past his lips. "Barely."

"On me," she whispered, as if the feel of his hot breath shocked her.

He pressed a kiss to her abdomen. Trailed his tongue down lower. And even lower.

"PJ!" Her whole body was quivering. Her fingers felt as if they were about to snatch him bald.

"Mmm." He gritted his teeth, nuzzled her with his nose.

"You can't! I'm not—I've never—"

"Of course you haven't." He raised his head, pressed one more quick kiss on her belly, then stretched out beside her, cradling her into his chest. "Next time."

"N-next?" Her voice was practically a squeak.

He smiled. "Oh, I think so. Yes."

But this time—her first time—he would take her there slowly and gently with all the care he was capable of, and he'd make every stop along the way.

He kissed her again, feathered light kisses over her shoulders, then up her neck to her face. He kissed her cheeks, her eyelids, the tip of her nose, her mouth.

And the kiss they'd shared that afternoon, startling though it had been, paled in the face of the kisses they shared now.

And the operative word was *sharing*. He wasn't the actor and she the "acted upon." Awkwardly but eagerly she kissed him back. Her hands roved over him, running down his back, tracing the line of his spine, sliding just for an instant beneath the waistband of the shorts he wore.

Shorts that were confining. Annoying. Shorts that he needed to shed. He sat up and made quick work of the skirt she had on, tugging it down over her hips and tossing it aside, then doing the same to his shorts.

As his erection lifted, eager and unconfined, he saw Ally's eyes widen. Her hand reached out as if she would touch him, then pulled back.

He settled back onto the bed again and stretched out next to her. "Go ahead."

She looked at him doubtfully. But then she lifted her hand and ran a single finger down the length of him.

It was his turn to arch and suck in a sharp breath.

Ally snatched her hand back. "Did I hurt you?"

"You didn't hurt me. It feels—" he shook his head, making a sound that wasn't quite a laugh "—wonderful."

Though it might kill him if he let her do it again.

"So, it's all right if I—" and she did it again, then circled him lightly with her fingers.

His breath came quick. His heart pounded. He bit his lip. "Maybe you'd better hold off a bit," he managed.

"I'm sorry. I didn't mean—" She looked stricken.

"It's okay," he assured her. "I like it. Too much. Let me…show you."

He might—possibly—be able to manage that. Giving Ally pleasure was just as exciting as having her touching him. More so, really. It was wondrous to watch her face as he stroked down her sides, as he circled her knees and trailed his fingers back up the insides of her thighs.

She moved restlessly, and he slid a thigh between her legs, opening her to his exploration. Ally's fingers gripped the sheets.

Her tongue slid between her lips as he slowly stroked closer and closer to the center of her.

He closed his eyes at the wet warmth he found there. He drew in a slow careful breath, smiling as he heard her suck in a much sharper one. He stroked deeper.

Her hips lifted. Her breath came fast. She gritted her teeth. "PJ! Oh, dear heavens!"

And he drew her into his arms as she shattered, too stunned to speak. He could feel her heart slamming against his, which had a serious staccato beat of its own. She was trembling as he kissed her, and then, still shaky, she pulled back.

"You," she whispered. "What about you?"

"Don't worry about me. I'm fine. Besides, we've got all night," PJ said. "That was for you."

He so much wanted to give Ally something. And, truthfully, the giving was the most amazing reward in itself.

But Ally wasn't content with that. She wanted to give to him, as well. Insisted on it. Soft hands stroked his body, learned his lines, his angles, his muscles even as he was learning hers.

And when he thought he might die for the mere pleasure of her fingers on him, she said, "Now, I think," and shifted her body, opened her thighs and urged him down between them.

PJ wanted to go slow, wanted to make it last. But the softness he eased into was heaven. The heat consumed him, raised him up, then burned him down at the same time.

"I can't—" he muttered. But he managed. Just. Eased in carefully. Held himself rigid. Excruciatingly still. Allowed Ally to adjust, to accommodate. To open to him, welcome him.

"Is this...all?" she whispered after a moment.

"All?" He almost laughed.

She moved experimentally, drew him deeper. A breath hissed between her teeth.

"Are you all right?" He could barely get the words out.

"I will be," Ally promised. She moved again. And again.

His own breath caught in his throat. "Ally!"

"Love me," she whispered and rocked her hips so that he felt again the tightness of her body around his.

That was all it took. Lose control? He had no control. Had nothing to lose but himself. And he did—in her.

He loved her eagerly, desperately, giving and taking simultaneously. They both did—caressing, stroking, touching, moving together until he had no idea where one of them ended and the other began.

It was only when Ally tumbled to sleep in his arms and he pulled back just enough to look at her sleeping face in the moonlight that spilled through the window that he felt the coolness of separation where the breeze touched his heated skin.

Ally didn't stir. Her black hair drifted against his pillow. He lifted a strand and touched it to his lips.

Then he'd just lain there, shattered, unable to tear his eyes from her, drinking in the sight, dazed and confused at having had a wedding night after all.

And wondering what the hell he had just done.

The intercom's buzz jolted him abruptly, and he realized he was standing at the window of his office, staring unseeing out at the Manhattan skyline.

There was no moonlight, no bed, no Ally.

He reached over and punched the button on the intercom. "What?"

"Ryne Murray is here."

"Give me a minute."

But a minute wasn't going to do it. He took a breath. Then another. Steadied himself. Or tried to. But his brain—and his body—were still focused on Ally.

Ally who was back.

Ally who was still his wife; who said she was in love with someone else.

But who kissed like she loved him.

* * *

Where was he?

Ally paced the length of the lobby for what seemed the hundredth time. It very well might have been.

She'd come downstairs at just past ten, having already paced around her room enough to wear a path in the carpet. Even though PJ wouldn't be there until noon, she'd needed to check out before eleven, and being around a lot of people and watching the passersby, she hoped would distract her, settle her down.

It didn't. A three ring circus underfoot wouldn't have distracted her. A herd of elephants tapdancing on Forty-second Street probably wouldn't have distracted her. She only thought about PJ—about spending the weekend with PJ—and grew more and more apprehensive.

She got a cup of coffee from the hospitality center. Having something in her hands would help. It would keep her from biting her fingernails, if nothing else. She sipped it and burned her tongue, muttered under her breath, paced some more.

She should have said she would meet him in the Hamptons. There were jitneys that traveled back and forth between the city and the Hamptons. She needn't have committed herself to a full afternoon in the car, just she and PJ.

But it was too late now.

She would have needed to make a reservation. And she would have had to tell him. And calling PJ was not on her list of things she wanted to do.

She knew he'd say, "Chicken, Al?"

And she wasn't. Really. She wasn't. Just…wary. Edgy. Nervous.

She would go through with it. Of course she would. But it would help if he would get here so she could stop fretting about it and start resisting.

"Ready?"

The sound of his voice right behind her made her jerk. Coffee splattered on the floor, on her shoes, on her shirt, on her hand.

"Oh!" She spun around and sloshed it on his shoes, too. "Stop sneaking up on me."

"I wasn't sneaking. You were walking away. I couldn't run around in front of you and say, 'Here I am,' could I? Are you okay?" He took the coffee out of her hand and set it down on a table while she tried ineffectually to mop herself up.

"I'm fine. Terrific. Never been better." She was muttering while she scrubbed at her shirt, then sighed and gave it up for a lost cause. "I need to change." She gave her still-stinging hand a shake.

"Let me see." PJ caught her fingers in his and examined her hand. It was red where the coffee had burned. But somehow the stinging from the burn was less intense than her awareness of his touch.

Abruptly Ally tried to pull her fingers away. But PJ held them fast and grimaced. "You should have some ice." He lifted his gaze, meeting hers. "And a kiss to make it better?" He grinned lopsidedly.

Ally snatched her hand out of his. "Ice, yes. A kiss, no."

"Don't want a repeat of last night, Al?" His tone was teasing.

But Ally had spent the night in far too deep a funk where kissing PJ was concerned. She compressed her lips. "I'll just get some ice and change my shirt and we can go."

Before he could reply, she took a fresh coral-colored pullover top from her suitcase, then, leaving the case with PJ, hurried to the ladies' room where she changed quickly, glared at her reflection in the mirror, exhorted herself to shape up, stay calm, cool and collected and, above all, resist PJ Antonides's charm.

Then she got a plastic bag of ice from the ice machine in the refreshment center, put it on her face before she put it on her hand. And then she made her way back to the lobby.

PJ had put her suitcase in his car—a late-model midsize SUV with a surfboard on the roof.

She stared at it. "I'll bet you're the only person in New York City with a surfboard on his car."

"I'm probably not," he said. "You'd be amazed at what you see in the city. How's your hand?" He opened the door for her and she climbed in, glad it was a good-size car and that she would be able to keep her distance.

"It'll be fine." She fastened her seat belt. He fastened his, then slid the car out into the crush of midtown noontime traffic.

Ally loved the city, but she never ever considered driving there. Honolulu was stress enough. But PJ maneuvered through the traffic as easily as he picked out and rode the waves he surfed.

"I become the wave," he'd told her once.

"Do you become the traffic?" she asked him now.

He slanted her a quick grin. "How'd you know?"

She resisted the grin and silently congratulated herself. "You make it look easy."

"I manage." He made a wry face. "It's not the most relaxing way to spend a Friday afternoon."

"You should have let me take one of the jitneys. I could have met you out there."

"No. I don't mind. Besides, it will give us a chance to spend some time together."

Precisely what Ally would have preferred not to have. But she said, "Yes. Are there going to be lots of people there?"

"Enough," PJ said grimly. "All the immediate family. The grandkids. My grandmother. A couple of my mother's sisters. One of my dad's crazy aunts. She's a widow, but her husband was the cousin of Ari Cristopolous, which is why my dad decided he could justify inviting them that weekend."

"But he really invited them because of…you…and the daughter?"

"Not that he'd ever admit it," PJ said cheerfully.

"Won't he be upset?"

PJ shrugged. "He knows now. Ma has to have told him. And he never stays upset long. He's pretty easygoing."

"But what about the Cristopolouses? And their daughter? Won't they be expecting…?"

"An unattached son?" PJ did a rapid tattoo with his fingers on the steering wheel, grinning. "Yep. Poor ol' Lukas."

Ally stared. "Lukas?"

"My little brother." PJ rolled his shoulders and sighed expansively. "Bless his heart."

Ally gave him a long skeptical look.

He just laughed. "Lukas won't mind. He never minds when people throw beautiful women at him."

"Do people often throw beautiful women at him?"

"Mostly beautiful women throw themselves at him. It's a little annoying." PJ shrugged. "They think he's good-looking. No accounting for taste. Tell me," he went on, "what happened yesterday at the gallery? With Gabriela del Castillo?"

Ally was curious about this brother whom women threw themselves at. It was hard to imagine anyone better looking than PJ. But then, maybe women threw themselves at him, too. She wanted to ask. But she didn't want to know. So she focused on the question he'd asked her.

"We had a really good meeting. I took half a dozen pieces— fabric art, quilted pieces, collages—and she accepted them all."

"Like what?"

"Oh, a couple of Thai beaches—very stylized. A couple of New Zealand ones. A bit of Polynesian Maori influence. And some landscape collage type things—a New York skyline at night."

One she didn't tell him about, was a much more personal piece—and one of the earliest she'd done. It had been her memories of the morning after the night they'd spent together, the view from his window toward the sea, the sand, the sunrise, the lone surfer on his board riding toward shore.

All the longing she'd felt that morning had gone into that piece. It had accompanied her everywhere. She'd shown it in several galleries, had had offers to buy it, had never sold. Couldn't bring herself to do it.

But she'd offered it for sale at Gaby's. She'd carried it with her too long. Like the marriage she was ending, it was time to part with it. So she'd told Gaby all the pieces she'd brought were for sale.

"I'm sending her more when I get home, and she's going to do a whole show—we're calling it Fabric of Our Lives."

PJ whistled. "That's fantastic." He seemed genuinely pleased. "Where is the gallery? What's it called?"

"Sol y Sombra Downtown. To distinguish it from another called Uptown she has on Madison Ave. Downtown is in Tribeca. The original is in Santa Fe."

Once she got talking about it, she couldn't seem to stop. And PJ encouraged her. He asked questions, listened to her replies, drew her out, seeming genuinely interested. And maybe because he was the only person to have shown any interest at all, she kept on going.

She told him about the other artists whose work she'd seen there. Gabriela del Castillo represented artists in a variety of mediums.

"I know what I like," she'd told Ally, "so that's what I represent."

She represented all sorts of oil and watercolor and acrylic artists as well as several photographers and a couple of sculptors.

"And she's just hung one room with work by a very talented muralist named Martha Antonides." It was her turn to flash a grin at him now. "I recognized your sister's work right away."

She had been as astonished to turn the corner in the gallery and find herself staring at an eight-foot-by-eight-foot painting that essentially took up a whole wall, a painting that captured summer in Central Park.

It was as if the artist had distilled the essence of New York's famous park—its zoo, its boats, its ball diamonds, fields, walkways and bike paths. The detail was incredible. Every person—and there were hundreds—was unique, special. Real.

And studying it while Gabriela went on at length about its

talented creator, Ally wished she'd gone back to look at the mural in PJ's apartment to find herself in it.

"Have you ever seen anything like it?" Gaby had asked eagerly.

"I have, actually," Ally had said. "I saw a couple of her murals earlier this week. She's amazingly talented."

"You can tell her so," PJ said when Ally repeated her comment to him. "She'll be delighted to hear it. I'm glad she's painting on something smaller than buildings these days. Easier for her, now that she's staying home with a kid."

It was easy to talk to PJ about her work and about his. And since his family figured largely in the company, she found that it was easy to ask about them. He talked readily, telling stories about growing up in a large boisterous family that made her laugh at the same time that she felt twinges of envy for the childhood he had known. It was so different from her own.

And while the thought of meeting a host of Antonideses was unnerving under the circumstances—she felt like a fraud—she found that the more she heard, the more eager she was to meet them.

More than once she said, "You're making that up," when PJ related some particularly outrageous anecdote, many of them having to do with things he and his brothers did or pranks he played on his sisters.

And every time he shook his head. "If you don't believe me, ask them."

"I will," she vowed.

The stories he told surprised her because PJ had always seemed distant from his family in Hawaii, determinedly so. But now he seemed to actually relish the time he spent with them.

"I thought you wanted to get away from your family," she remarked as they headed east through one suburb after another until finally they got far enough beyond the city that there were actually cultivated fields and open spaces here and there.

The sun was shining. A breeze lifted her hair. The summer heat that had been oppressive in the city was appealing out here.

"I did," PJ said. The wind was tousling his hair, too. "They're great in small doses. Like this weekend. But I needed to be on my own. So I left. To find myself. Like you did," he added, glancing her way.

She hadn't thought about that before. She'd been so consumed by her own life in those days that she hadn't really thought about what motivated anyone else. PJ's proposal had been a favor, but had always seemed more of a casual, "Oh well, I'm not marrying anyone else this week," sort of thing.

She hadn't realized that he'd equated her situation with his own.

"Did you realize that then?" she asked.

"It occurred to me." He kept his eyes on the road.

Ally turned her eyes on him, understanding a bit better what had motivated him. Which should, she reminded herself, make it easier to resist the attraction she felt.

She'd been a "cause" for him then. Nothing more, nothing less. And this weekend her chance to pay him back. On Sunday he would take her back to the city. Monday she would catch a plane back to her real life.

And what PJ told his family afterward was not her problem. But the weekend could be a problem unless they discussed it ahead of time.

She turned to PJ. "Before we arrive, we need to get a few things straight."

CHAPTER SEVEN

"WHAT sort of things?" PJ slanted her a wary glance.

She had seen signs for various Hamptons—West Hampton, Bridgehampton, East Hampton—so she knew they were getting near now. She didn't know which PJ's parents lived in, but the knowledge that she'd be meeting them soon banished her pleasure at the surprising ease of the journey and was replaced by jittery nerves and a definite edginess.

"Rules," she said.

"Rules?" he repeated, sounding incredulous. "What sort of rules?"

"No kissing."

His head jerked around. Disbelieving green eyes stared at her. "What?"

"You heard me," she said, feeling her cheeks begin to heat.

"Not right, I didn't," PJ muttered under his breath. "I'm your husband," he reminded her.

"Only for the moment," she said primly.

"You can kiss me like you did and still want a divorce?"

Now her face really was burning. "You caught me off guard. And I never said you weren't appealing. It's just..." she hesitated. There was no way she could discuss this with him. They weren't speaking the same language. "I won't say that I'm filing for divorce. I'll leave that up to you."

"Big of you," he muttered. His fingers tightened on the steering wheel. His knuckles were white.

"I just—" she plucked at the hem of her skirt "—don't think we should lead them to expect that we're a couple."

"Ally, in their eyes we *are* a couple. We're married."

"I shouldn't have come."

"Well, too bad. You're here now," PJ said as he flipped on the turn signal and, the next thing Ally knew, they were off the highway and heading south. She clenched her fists in her lap and tried to settle her nerves. She took a deep breath intended to calm her.

"You're not going underwater," PJ said. "Relax. They don't bite. I don't either," he added grimly.

"You kiss," Ally muttered.

"And damn well, or so I've been told," he retorted, then tipped his head to angle a look at her. "You didn't seem to have any complaints."

"You kiss very well," she said primly, staring straight ahead. "And you've proved that."

He made another right turn, then a left. They were getting closer and closer to the shore, running out of houses. And she was running out of time. She turned to entreat him. "I don't want us to make this any more difficult than it is, PJ."

He slowed the car and looked straight at her. "I didn't realize it was such a terrible imposition."

"It's not! It's—" she couldn't explain. She couldn't even make sense of her tangled feelings herself "—not difficult. But it is awkward. I feel like a fraud. That's why I don't want kissing."

He let the car roll to a stop now. They were sitting in the middle of the road. Fortunately there was no traffic. He let his hands lie loosely on the steering wheel for a long moment before he drew a long breath, then said quietly, "Is it when you kiss *me* that you feel like a fraud, Ally?"

He didn't wait for her to answer. He gunned the engine and they shot down the road another hundred yards and then he swung the car into a large paved parking area behind an immense stone and timber pseudo-English-style two-story house.

"Home sweet home," he said, and without glancing her way, he hopped out of the car.

Challenged by PJ's question, Ally sat right where she was, feeling as if she'd just taken a body blow to the gut. But before she could even face the question internally, let alone articulate a reply to PJ, he jerked open the door on her side of the car and said tersely, "Come and meet my parents."

Knees wobbling, and not just from being stuck in a car too long, Ally got out. She wasn't sure exactly what she'd expected—apart from being nervous—when he introduced her to his parents. Probably she hadn't even let herself think that far.

But whatever fleeting notions she had, they didn't come close to what she got.

"Good luck with your 'no kissing' rule," PJ said just before he turned to face the horde of relatives descending upon them.

And the next instant, they were surrounded.

"Ma, Dad, this is Ally. Al, these are my parents, Aeolus and Helena," PJ said and somehow he swept them together.

And instead of politely shaking hands and saying, "How do you do?" as Ally had expected, she was instantly enveloped in Aeolus's hearty embrace, her cheeks were kissed, her body was squeezed, her hands were pumped.

"And so you are real!" he said jovially, dark eyes flashing with humor. "My boy is just full of surprises!"

And somehow he managed to wrap PJ into the same fierce hug so that she might not have kissed him, but she certainly had plenty of body contact before Aeolus struck again, this time drawing his wife into their midst.

PJ's mother was not quite as effusive as her husband. But her expression, though clearly inquisitive, was warm and her smile was just as welcoming.

"A new daughter," she murmured, taking Ally's cheeks

between her palms and looking straight into her eyes. "How wonderful."

And just as she was smitten by guilt, Ally was kissed with gentle warmth. Then Helena stepped back, still smiling and slid an arm around Ally's waist, drawing her away from PJ and his father. "Come," she said, "and meet your family."

Her family.

More guilt. More dismay. And yet, how could she not smile and allow herself to be passed from one to another. There were so many, all dark-haired, eager and smiling, as they shook her hand, kissed her cheeks, told her their names.

Some names she recognized—PJ's siblings, Elias and Martha, their spouses and a swarm of little boys who must be more of PJ's nephews. There was another brother, some aunts, cousins, friends.

She heard Mr. and Mrs. Cristopolous's names, but they were just part of the blur. She did get a bead on Connie, though, the woman Aeolus hoped his son would marry.

Connie Cristopolous was the most perfectly beautiful woman Ally had ever seen. She was blessed with naturally curling black hair. Ally's own, stick straight, couldn't compare. Not only did it curl, but it actually seemed to behave itself instead of flying around the way most of the women's hair did. Her complexion was smooth and sun touched. Her features— a small neat nose, full smiling lips, deep brown eyes—were perfect. And she had just enough cheekbone to give her face memorable definition, but enough fullness in her cheeks to make her face warm and feminine.

She smiled at Ally and greeted her warmly. "So glad to meet Peter's wife," she said in a lightly accented voice that reminded Ally of the spread of warm honey. Even her thick luxuriant eyelashes were perfect.

Maybe she was a perfect shrew, too. But somehow Ally doubted it. PJ's father didn't look like the sort of man who would have chosen a shrew as a potential daughter-in-law. Ally suspected Aeolus Antonides had terrific taste in women.

She slanted a quick glance at PJ, who was being mobbed by his aunts and mauled by his brothers. He didn't seem to be noticing Connie. But no doubt he would.

Maybe he would even marry her. After all, she could be his, once the divorce was final.

The thought made Ally stiffen involuntarily, and she narrowed her gaze at the other woman, as if she could discern at a glance whether she was worthy of a man like PJ. Would she love him?

Would he love *her?*

The question made Ally stumble as she was being led up the steps to the house by a couple of PJ's aunts.

"Are you all right, dear?" one asked her, catching her by the elbow to make sure she didn't fall.

"F-fine," Ally stammered. But she wasn't all right. The truth was that while she might be able to cope with the idea that PJ didn't really love her, she didn't want him falling in love with anyone else, either.

Mortifying, but true.

"Come and meet *Yiayia.*" The aunts drew her into the house.

The house PJ had grown up in was as lovely and warm within as it was without. There was a lot of dark wood paneling, floor-to-ceiling bookcases and a massive field-stone fireplace, which could have been oppressive but was softened by overstuffed sofas and chairs and balanced and lightened by high ceilings and French doors. These faced south and opened onto a deck that led to a lawn, then down a flight of wooden steps to the sand—and the ocean and horizon beyond.

Ally, seeing that, felt a moment's peace. She would have preferred to stop there, admire and take a breath, try to regain her equilibrium.

But the aunts were towing her on through the dining room and into the kitchen where a small still-dark-haired elderly lady was in the middle of a rather elaborate baking project. Her hands were stuck in something that looked like honey and ground nuts. A very sticky business.

Ally wondered how they would handle the requisite hug.

But though the older woman looked up when they came in, her eyes, bright and curious as they lit on Ally, she made no move to take her hands out of the bowl. She simply looked Ally over.

It was clear she needed no introduction to the new arrival. She was already assessing her carefully. She did not smile.

And Ally, who was still feeling overwhelmed, was almost grateful. And her gratitude had nothing to do with avoiding the sticky stuff.

"This is *Yiayia,*" one of the aunts said. "Grandma," she translated in case Ally couldn't.

Ally could. PJ hadn't said much about his grandmother. He'd indicated that she would be there, but nothing more.

She smiled at the old woman who didn't smile back. She was still studying Ally closely and in complete silence. Ally wondered suddenly if PJ's grandmother spoke English.

Well, if she didn't, they'd certainly figure out another way to communicate. The family seemed big on kisses and hugs. At least, all of them but Grandma.

"Hello," she said at last, when it was clear that PJ's grandmother wasn't going to take the conversational lead. "I'm so glad to meet you. I'm Alice. Or Ally if you prefer. Or Al if you're PJ," she added with a small conspiratorial grin, inviting PJ's grandmother to share a grin with her.

She was surprised to discover how very much she wanted the old lady to smile.

"Alice," PJ's grandmother said quietly at last, her gaze still fastened on Ally's face. But even then her expression didn't change. She turned and looked up at the aunts. "Alice will help me. Go now."

They looked at her, then at Ally, then at each other and, with only that much hesitation, they nodded and left.

Outside Ally could hear a multitude of voices, laughter,

scuffling. But no one came into the kitchen. In the kitchen it was just she and PJ's grandmother. It felt like having an audience with the pope.

Like going to see her own father who was distant and formal and also rarely ever smiled. Ally almost breathed a little easier. This was more what she expected.

And then suddenly the door opened and PJ strode into the room. At the sight his grandmother burst into an absolutely radiant smile. And when he crossed the room in three long strides to pick her up bodily, sticky hands and all, and kiss her soundly, she crowed with laughter, then put her honey-coated hands on each of his cheeks and kissed him right back.

Ally felt her mouth drop open.

Both PJ and his grandmother turned toward her. "So, what do you think of my wife, *Yiayia?*" he said. "Isn't she gorgeous?"

"A beauty," his grandmother agreed. She was still smiling, still patting his cheek with her sticky hand but her eyes were shrewd when they met Ally's. "So, this is Alice." It sounded like a pronouncement.

PJ nodded. He was still smiling, but there was a serious-ness in his expression that told Ally something else was under-neath the smile.

"You went to get her?"

"She came to me."

"Ah." His grandmother's brows lifted. Her gaze softened a bit, a hint of a smile touched her face. "*Ne.* This is better."

Better? Than what? Ally could tell there was a subtext to the conversation, but neither PJ nor his grandmother enlightened her. And all the vibes she was getting said it wasn't better at all. She was very much afraid that PJ's grandmother, like his sister Cristina, was misunderstanding the situation.

"So, you have come," the old lady said, approvingly. "At last."

"Don't give her a hard time, *Yiayia.* She's had things to do."

"More important than her husband?"

"Important for her," PJ said firmly. "Like when I went to Hawaii for school. That was important for me. You understand?"

The old lady eyed him narrowly for a long moment, then slanted a gaze of silent judgment at Ally, who stood motionless and didn't say a word.

"*Ne*. I understand, yes," she said. She sighed. "You are happy now?"

PJ grinned. "Of course I'm happy now." He took her fingers and nibbled the honey off each one, making her laugh again. "Why wouldn't I be? I've got two of my favorite women right here in the room with me. You're making baklava." He nodded at the project underway on the counter. Then he sniffed the air. "Mom's made roast for dinner. And there's no way Dad can foist any more women off on me."

His grandmother laughed, reassured. "Wash your face and go help your brother with his twins. Tallie must put her feet up and rest. She's going to be a mother again."

"Really?" PJ was clearly delighted. "When?"

"In the spring. Go now. Leave your wife," she said after he'd washed his hands and face and had turned toward Ally. "Alice and I will talk."

"But—"

"Go," his grandmother ordered. "Trust me. I will not eat her."

Still he hesitated for a moment. "She's worse than Cristina," he said to Ally. There was a warning look on his face.

"We'll be fine. I've always wanted to learn how to make baklava."

Yiayia smiled and nodded. "I will teach you."

"Just be sure that's all you do," PJ warned his grandmother. He dropped another kiss on her forehead, then with a quick smile at Ally, went out the door, yelling for Elias.

They both watched him go. Then as she cleaned her hands and began to layer the filo and melted butter with the honey mixture, PJ's grandmother said something in Greek.

"I'm sorry. I didn't understand," Ally said, coming closer

and picking up the brush to help butter the layers as *Yiayia* spread them out.

"I said," *Yiayia* repeated clearly, in English this time, "he is my favorite."

She smiled fondly out the window where they could both see PJ rescuing his older brother who was being used as a human climbing frame by his toddler-aged twins. "All of my grandchildren I love, *ne?* But Peter I love the most." She turned to Ally and shook her head.

"I don't say that to anyone else," she went on. "But I know. He knows. He is the most like my dear Aeneas. Strong and gentle like his grandfather. He makes me laugh. He makes me happy. He is a good man."

"Yes." Ally knew that. She'd always known it.

"A man who deserves to be happy, too," *Yiayia* added.

"Yes."

"He says he is."

"I hope he is," Ally agreed quickly, then felt more was needed. "I want him to be happy," she said fervently. And that was the truth. "I know he was happy to come home for the weekend."

"Now that you are here and his father knows what he says is true. But that is not what I mean. He says he is happy, but I wonder…" Her voice trailed off and her gaze turned to the windows again as she watched PJ and Elias on the lawn playing with the little boys. They all were laughing.

"He looks happy," Ally said stoutly.

"*Ne.*" *Yiayia* agreed, nodding. "But then I ask myself—" she looked archly at Ally over her spectacles "—why does a man who is happy and in love, kiss his old wrinkled *yiayia* and not his lovely wife?"

As tough as the old woman was, Ally liked her.

She felt guilty for not confessing her plans. But she'd promised PJ she wouldn't mention the divorce. And the truth was, even if she hadn't promised, she wasn't sure she could have got the words past her lips.

It felt like a sacrilege to even think it, much less bring it up. And she completely forgot about it after another ten minutes of conversation, during which PJ's grandmother changed the subject and asked about her art and her retail business.

Her questions weren't casual. They demonstrated she was not only knowledgeable but that PJ had obviously told her a great deal about what Ally did.

"He is very proud of you," she said.

"He made it possible."

Yiayia smiled. "And now you make him happy." Her eyes met Ally's over the pan of baklava. They were back to "happy" again. And this time *Yiayia*'s words very definitely held a challenge.

But before she could figure out how to respond, PJ's grandmother said, "Here comes Martha. You will love Martha."

And as she spoke, the door from the deck swung open and Martha stuck her head in. She carried her toddler son on her hip.

"Oh, good, you are here," she said to Ally. "I've been looking for you." Then, "Can you spare her, *Yiayia?* I want to get acquainted with my sister-in-law."

When they'd first met, Martha had simply beamed and kissed her. Was she now about to grill Ally the way PJ's grandmother and Cristina had?

But before she could demur, *Yiayia* said, "You go, both of you. Hurry now, Martha, or your mother will put you to work."

"God forbid." Martha laughed. "Come on," she said to Ally. "We'll go down on the beach. Eddie can eat sand."

She led the way and, bemused, Ally followed.

"I saw one of your murals at Sol Y Sombra," she told Martha. "It was amazing."

And any concern she might have had about Martha's reaction to her relationship with PJ evaporated right then. Martha's face lit up. "You were there?" And when Ally explained, her eyes widened. "Gaby's showing your work, too?"

She was clearly delighted and peppered Ally with a thousand questions—about her art, about her shops, about her focus. And she was absolutely thrilled to meet PJ's wife.

"Dad didn't think you really existed," she confided. "It's so cool to discover you do. And even cooler that I like you!"

If Cristina had been suspicious, Martha was just the opposite. She was eager to welcome Ally into the family. She practically danced along the beach as they followed Eddie from one pile of flotsam and jetsam to another.

"We'll have to get together. Maybe in Santorini—or we could come to Hawaii sometime, Theo and Eddie and I," she said, eyes alight with possibilities. "Theo would love that. He sails. He and PJ bonded over PJ's windsurfer. They have a lot in common. And apparently we do, too."

And what was Ally supposed to say? No, they didn't?

"That would be fun," she managed. And she was telling the truth when she said it. It would be absolutely wonderful, if only…

Something of her hesitation must have shown through, because Martha immediately said, "Don't let me bully you into it. Theo is always telling me I shouldn't just assume."

"No," Ally said quickly. "I really would love it. I just… We don't know what we're doing yet, PJ and I. We have to…discuss things."

"Of course," Martha said quickly. "It must be so weird, getting back together after all these years."

Ally nodded. "We don't really know each other…"

"Why did you stay away so long?"

And how, Ally wondered, could she even begin to answer that?

"There always seemed to be things to do," she said, "and PJ married me so I could do them." She knew that all the Antonides clan had heard the story of her grandmother's legacy by now. But she didn't know how much else any of them knew. She shrugged and turned to stare out to sea. It was easier that way than when she had to look into Martha's face. "And once I finally got going, I was a success. I ended up on a fast track.

Doing what he'd expected me to do. And—" she shrugged "—as that was what we'd married for, I just…kept doing it. I guess I thought he would have moved on. Got a divorce."

"Could he?"

Ally nodded. "If he had filed and I didn't respond, yes. He could have got a divorce without my ever having to sign anything."

"Bet you're glad he didn't. Bet he is, too." Martha shook her head. "Wow. What if you'd come back and found out you were already divorced? What if he'd married somebody else?" She looked appalled at the thought.

And Ally had to admit to a certain jolt when she thought about it, too. Of course it would have been easier. She could have married Jon without any of this ever happening.

"You wouldn't be here now," Martha said, making almost exactly the same mental leaps. Then she laughed. "And PJ would be facing a weekend with Connie Cristopolous."

"She's beautiful," Ally protested.

"But not PJ's type."

Ally wasn't sure what PJ's type was. But before she could ask Martha's opinion, the other woman went on, "So how did you find him?"

And Ally told her about going back to Honolulu, about her dad's heart attack, about looking for PJ. "I thought he'd be there still," she admitted. "But he wasn't."

"And so you had to track him down! How romantic is that?" Martha was clearly pleased.

Cristina thought PJ was the romantic. Martha thought she was.

"Eddie! Ack, no. Don't put that in your mouth!" Martha swooped down and scooped her son up, taking whatever he'd been about to eat and tossing it into the water. "Kids! What will I ever do when I have two of them?" she moaned.

"Are you…?" Ally looked at Martha's flat stomach doubtfully.

But Martha nodded happily. "Not till January, though. What about you guys? Have you talked about kids?"

"Not…much."

It wasn't exactly a lie. They had talked about children—the ones she hoped to have with Jon, the grandchild she wanted to give her father.

But now in her mind's eye she didn't see a child she might have with Jon. She saw PJ as he had been with Alex that evening at his house in Park Slope or, for that matter, PJ now. He had one of Elias's twins on his hip while he tossed a football with his brothers.

Martha's gaze followed her own. "Well, it's early days yet. You will."

Ally didn't reply. Her throat felt tight. The glare of the sun made her eyes water. She swallowed and looked away.

As a child, Ally had been a reader.

From the time she had first made sense of words on a page, she'd haunted the library or spent her allowance at the bookstore, buying new worlds in which to live. And invariably the worlds she sought were the boisterous chaotic worlds of laughing, loving, noisy families who were so different from her own.

Oh, she was loved. She had no doubt about that.

But the everyday life of her childhood had been perpetually calm, perennially quiet, perfectly ordered. When her mother had been alive, there had, of course, been smiles and quiet laughter. And even her normally dignified taciturn father had been known to join in. But after her mother's death, after the number of chairs at the table had gone from three to two, mealtimes had become sober silent affairs. After her mother was gone, there had been no more light conversations, no more gentle teasing. There had actually been very few smiles.

Never a demonstrative man, after his wife's death Hiroshi Maruyama became even more remote.

"He is sad," her grandmother had excused him.

"So am I," Ally had retorted fiercely. "Does he think I don't miss her, too?"

"He doesn't think," Ama had said. "He only hurts."

Well, Ally had hurt, too. And they had gone right on hurting in their own private little shells, never reaching out for each other, for years. Hiroshi's way of dealing with his daughter was to give her directions, orders, commands.

"They will make your life better," he told her stiffly, if she balked.

But they hadn't.

Marrying PJ and running away from her father's edicts was what had made her life better. Doing that had freed her, given her scope for her talents, new challenges that she could meet and, eventually, a life she loved and determinedly filled with her art and her work.

In the fullness of that life, she'd forgotten about the warm, boisterous families she'd read about and envied, the closeness she had yearned for all those years ago. She hadn't really realized anything was missing until she'd come home after her father's heart attack.

Then, forced to take a break, to slow down and look around during those long days in his hospital room, she had seen cracks in her well-developed life begin to appear. A chasm of emptiness opened up before her.

She was back with her father—in subdued silence. And longing for something more. That was why she'd been so glad to find Jon.

He was as addicted to work as she was. For his entire adult life he had been filling the empty spaces in his life with patients and professional demands on his time. Now he was thirty-five. It was time to marry, to have a family.

"One child," he said. "I have time for one child."

"Two," Ally had responded instantly. "I want at least two." There was no way she was going to subject a child of hers to the same loneliness she'd experienced.

Jon had looked doubtful and skeptical and as if he thought she was being irrational and irresponsible.

"Two," Ally had repeated. "Or three," she'd added in a moment of recklessness.

"No more than two," Jon had stated firmly. "We don't want chaos."

But a part of Ally did.

And tonight on the deck of PJ's parents' house, she was reminded of it.

The whole day, from the moment she'd got out of the car to be swept into the embrace of his parents, siblings, aunts, uncles, cousins and assorted relations, she had felt a sense of déjà vu that was odd because she knew she'd never experienced anything like it before.

It wasn't until after dinner, when she'd sat on a bench on the deck listening to Martha and Tallie compare toddler notes while in the kitchen the aunts discussed recipes, and in the dining room PJ's father, Mr. Cristopolous and several friends compared golf swings and on the lawn little boys toddled about and bigger boys tossed footballs, and on the sand where PJ's brother Lukas was deep in conversation with Connie Cristopolous and PJ and Elias were starting up a bonfire in the rock fire pit that Ally recognized what she was seeing—the families she'd read about in her books.

They were real—at least this one was. And for the moment—for this one single weekend—they were hers.

She smiled. Not just on her face, but all the way down to the depths of her soul.

"Come on, then, Ally." Martha broke into her realization. "I'll show you guys the mural I'm doing in Ma's sewing room."

And happily, willingly, Ally went with Martha and Tallie. She ran her hand along the oak banister as they climbed the stairs, certain that the wood beneath her fingers had been worn smooth by PJ and his brothers sliding down it. She paused to look at the family photos that lined the upstairs hall. They stretched back for generations, right to a couple of fiercely scowling men with bushy moustaches who looked as if they'd just got off the boat.

"My great-grandfather Nikos and his brother, right after

they emigrated," Martha said when she noticed the direction of Ally's glance. "I want to do a mural of the whole family—" she waved her hand to encompass the myriad photos on both the walls "—sometime. Show all the generations. I did something like it out in Butte as a local history project. You would have loved this photo of a traditional Chinese bride one of the students brought in."

Martha rattled on happily about that, while Ally and Tallie admired the ongoing mural in Helena's sewing room. Martha had done small vignettes of children—the Antonides children. Here was Alex throwing a ball, Eddie taking his first steps, the twins smearing birthday cake all over their faces. And their parents, too, when they were children. All of Helena's and Aeolus's children were there.

"Is that PJ?" Ally asked, arrested by a small painting on the wall by the bay window of a young boy on a surfboard.

Martha laughed. "Who else?"

Who else, indeed? Ally moved closer, drawn to the picture of PJ as a boy, recognizing the triumphant grin and, in his expression, the sheer joy of being alive.

"Of all of us kids," Martha said, "he was the one who loved it here the most. The one who loved the ocean the most. We always thought he was insane, going all the way to Hawaii when he had one out the back door. But—" she smiled at Ally "—I guess he wasn't so crazy after all. Look who he brought home."

And there was such warmth and such approval in her voice that Ally felt about two inches high.

She couldn't respond to it, could only smile and feel betraying tears prick.

"Hey," PJ's voice came from the doorway. "I wondered where you'd got to."

"Brought her up to show her family history," Martha said. "You haven't seen this, either." She waved a hand around the room.

PJ ambled in and startled Ally by snagging her hand and drawing her along with him while he moved from vignette to vignette. She tried to look at them, too, but mostly she was aware of his hand wrapping hers.

She should tug it away. It was sending the wrong message, and not just to the onlookers, but to Ally herself. It promised a relationship, a future. A married life of love.

Experimentally she tried pulling her hand out of his. He hung on tighter. "They're terrific," he told Martha, nodding at her paintings. "Ma loves 'em. Says she's going to make you fill the whole room."

"Yes, well, Theo and I are doing our part. Tallie and Elias are doing theirs. Up to you now," she added giving him a significant look.

Ally tensed at her obvious inference, but PJ's grip on her hand didn't change. "All in good time," he said easily. Then, as if he took it all in stride, as doubtless he did, he said to all of them, "Fire's going. Sun's set. Come on out."

The scene around the firepit was even more reminiscent of all the stories she used to read. Most of the family gathered around it, sitting on blankets, laughing and talking as the evening lengthened and the sky grew deep and dark.

The breeze off the ocean turned the air cool, and Ally would have gone for her sweater, but before she could, PJ slipped his sweatshirt jacket over her shoulders.

"Come here," he said, and drew her down onto the blanket, shifting around so that she sat in the vee of his legs and he tugged her back against his chest, looping his arms around her.

It felt far too intimate for Ally's peace of mind. But at the same time, perversely, it felt like exactly where she wanted to be.

"Warmer?" His lips were next to her ear, his breath lifting tendrils of her hair.

She shivered again at the feel of it and, misunderstanding the cause, he wrapped his arms more tightly around her. "I can go get you a warmer jacket."

It would have got her out of his arms. Saying "Yes, please" would have been the sane thing to do, but Ally didn't do it.

She couldn't bring herself to destroy the evening. It was her dream come to life. The warmth and joy of the camaraderie, the laughter and easy music that began as Lukas picked up a guitar and began to play, and two of PJ's aunts began to sing, enchanted her. And the hard strength of PJ's arms around her simply enhanced the experience.

"I'm fine," she said.

It was true. It was wonderful.

It lasted the rest of the night.

It was late when the party began to break up. Tallie and Elias had put the twins down to sleep. Martha had gone inside to rock Eddie. *Yiayia* had gone up to bed an hour earlier, but not before she'd stopped on her way in to smile down at Ally, snug in the embrace of PJ's arms.

"Ne," she said approvingly. And her fingers had brushed over the top of Ally's head. A benediction of sorts?

"Night, *Yiayia*," PJ said, tilting his head up to smile at her.

Yiayia said something to him in Greek that Ally didn't understand. She was surprised when PJ seemed to.

His smile broadened and he nodded. "Don't worry," he said. "I will."

His grandmother nodded and padded off into the house.

"What did she say?" Ally wanted to know.

"She said I shouldn't forget to kiss you."

Ally's breath caught in her throat, knowing that PJ's lips were a scant inch from her ear. But even as she held her breath, he made no move to kiss her.

Instead he eased back away from her and stood up, then held out a hand and hauled her to her feet. "Time to go up," he said.

"Yes. It is late. Nearly midnight." She felt stiff from having sat there so long, yet she was reluctant to leave. Lukas was still softly playing his guitar. And Connie, apparently oblivious to any machinations that would have directed her toward PJ, seemed enthralled with sitting at Lukas's feet and listening to his music. Elias and Tallie had come back out and were sitting on the other side of the fire, their arms around each other as they stared into the magic of the fire.

Ally understood. She didn't want to leave the magic, either.

But she could do exactly what she'd always done as a child after she'd read one of those books that made her dream impossible dreams. She could take her dreams to bed with her.

But first, she reminded herself as she followed PJ up the stairs so he could show her to her room, she should call Jon.

She hadn't called him all day. But it wasn't too late. With the time difference, he would probably just be getting home from the hospital. Maybe she could communicate a little of what she'd felt today to him—this feeling of family belonging, joy, connection. Maybe he would understand.

Maybe, she dared hope, he would share her dream.

PJ took hold of the handle on one of the doors in the hallway. "Here we are." He pushed the door open and held it for her. "My old room," he said with a grin.

"Yours?" She looked around, intrigued. It had obviously been redecorated since PJ had lived in it. The walls were a freshly painted pale sage green. But the bookcase still had some books that the young PJ Antonides would have read, and the hardwood floors showed evidence of being used for more than walking.

"Used to have bunkbeds, too," he told her. There was a double-size bed in the room now, with a taupe-colored duvet and heaps of inviting pillows. "I had the top one. Always wanted to be on top. Luke was stuck with the bottom."

She could imagine him in here, her mind's eye seeing the boy on the surfboard that Martha had painted. She wondered about the dreams he had dreamed as a child. He needn't have dreamed ones like hers. They'd been his reality.

Then she realized he was just standing there looking at her. "What?" she said.

He shook his head, smiling, too. "Nothing." But still he made no move to go.

"Where are you going to be?" she asked him.

He blinked. "What?"

She shrugged. "I just wondered where you were sleeping? Which room?"

"This one," he said. "I'm sleeping in here. With you."

CHAPTER EIGHT

PJ WAITED for the inevitable, "No!" and the predictable protest that would follow.

Ally stood stock-still in the middle of the bedroom, staring at him, her eyes wide, looking stricken. She opened her mouth, and he prepared himself for the argument, the refusal, for more of her damn "rules."

Then just as abruptly her mouth closed again.

Her expression shifted subtly, becoming unreadable. Or at least unreadable to him.

Ten years ago Ally Maruyama had been an open book. Serious and sunny by turns, yes, but still fathomable. PJ had always understood where she was coming from, what she hoped for, what her dreams were.

This Ally was as fathomable as cement.

She kissed him like she wanted him. Hell, the way she'd responded to his kisses had nearly burned him to the ground. And she hadn't been immune, either. That much he did know.

And yet she persisted in wanting the divorce.

And now she was looking at him, not saying anything. Just looking.

"I suppose you think I should have got you a separate bedroom," he said gruffly, scowled as he deliberately began unbuttoning his shirt.

"No," she said with maddening calm. "I'm sure that would

have been awkward. Your mother would definitely have asked questions. I guess it just…didn't occur to me. I'm an idiot." Then she shrugged as if it didn't matter. And damned if she didn't just take hold of the hem of her shirt and pull it over her head!

PJ's mouth went dry. She wasn't going to kiss him, but she'd strip for him? God Almighty.

She wasn't baring anything yet that she couldn't bare in public. Beneath her top she had on a lacy ivory bra. It was at least as discreet as any bikini top. But he hadn't seen her breasts, even in that state of coverage in ten years. He remembered them as small ripe handfuls that had begged to be kissed. Now they were fuller, riper. A woman's breasts.

And he needed to kiss them again—now.

Like a slow fire, his desire had been simmering all day. From the minute he'd spotted her in the hotel lobby, he'd felt a quickening in his pulse, an awareness that he never felt with any other woman. He'd told himself it was just the heat of the moment, that it would fade.

But the trip out to the Hamptons hadn't really dampened it. Talking with her, listening to her, finding out more about who she'd become after all these years—even when they were doing nothing more than that—actually seemed to deepen his awareness of her.

Seeing her with his family had made it deeper still.

If she'd been stiff and silent, treating them with distant politeness, he would have backed off. But even though she'd looked a bit overwhelmed at times, she'd slipped into the pool of Antonides family warmth and hadn't come close to drowning.

She'd talked sailing with his father, canning tomatoes with his mother, and had been thrilled to discuss quilting with his aunts Narcissa and Maria. She and his brother Lukas had compared notes about riding camels in the outback of Australia. From the shy girl she'd been when he'd first met her, she had clearly blossomed. She seemed to enjoy them all.

And he knew they had enjoyed her. Even his grandmother,

whose reaction he'd been a little wary of, truth to tell, had warmed to her.

She'd taken him by the arm after dinner and said, "You surprise me, Petros."

And he'd stiffened because he didn't want to hear what she might have to say. "How so?" he'd demanded, a bit more belligerent than he usually was with his grandmother whom he adored.

"You swim in deep waters."

He'd frowned and narrowed his gaze. "What are you talking about, *Yiayia?*"

"Your wife."

Which was exactly what he'd been afraid they were talking about. "Don't be cryptic," he'd told her. "If you've got something to say, just spit it out. Not that it's going to make a damn bit of difference," he'd added gruffly.

Her brows had lifted. Dark eyes bored into his. A small smile touched her face. "You have it bad," she'd said.

"I have a wife," he'd retorted.

"A beautiful wife," she agreed. "A strong wife. But a wife, I think, who is still finding her way. *Ne,* Petros?"

His jaw had tightened. He'd lifted his shoulders slightly. He didn't speak.

He hadn't had to. *Yiayia* had always known what he was thinking, had always known what was important to him. She'd put her small but still-strong fingers over his and squeezed.

"I like her," she'd said. "Your Ally is honest. When she knows the truth, so will you."

What he knew right now, staring at Ally in her bra and capri pants, was confusion.

"What happened to the 'no kissing' business?" he said hoarsely.

She was rummaging in her suitcase, taking out some sort of nightshirt that didn't look very sexy at all but still managed to make his blood hot. At his question, she turned, looking over her shoulder at him. "Nothing happened to it."

"We're going to sleep in the same bed all night and nothing's going to happen?"

She turned and straightened. "Well, I suppose you could force yourself on me." The look she gave him was a defiant challenge.

His breath hissed through his teeth. "You know damned well I won't do that."

"I didn't think you would." She picked up the nightshirt and a toiletries bag and headed toward the bathroom, saying as off-handedly as she could manage, "I'm going to grab a quick shower. I'll be right back."

And she left him with his jaw dropped, his mouth dry and his body—well, his body could do with a shower, too.

A long ice-cold one.

Someone—probably PJ, come to think of it—had once said, "The best defense is a good offense."

Ally understood the concept. And she knew it applied to football and war. Neither her father nor Jon had any experience with either. So she was certain they hadn't said it. In fact she thought she could remember the instant PJ had branded the words on her brain.

"Stop running from your old man's edicts," he'd told her that fateful afternoon ten years ago. "Face him down. The best defense is a good offense," he'd added. Or words to that effect.

And then he'd proved it by asking her to marry him.

The same words had popped into her mind a few seconds after PJ's words, "I'm sleeping in here. With you," reached her ears.

Her first reaction, of course, was to argue with him. But they'd been there, done that. And doing it again wasn't going to settle anything, much less clarify their relationship.

And sleeping with him is? Ally asked herself sarcastically as she confronted her naked image in the bathroom mirror.

She didn't know the answer to that. But she wanted to know. And somehow as risky as that was, it seemed a better way to do it than go down the same path of argument again, she told herself as she finished drying off and pulled on her nightshirt.

He'd touched a nerve when he'd challenged her about when exactly it was that she felt like a fraud. Because, truth to tell, she felt something strong and vital when she was kissing PJ, and it was a feeling she had not yet captured with Jon. There was sweetness in kissing Jon, a sense of connection.

But nothing like the soul-searing full-on connection she seemed to feel with PJ.

And today everything that happened had only made those feelings—that connection—more intense, on levels that had nothing to do with kissing.

Maybe it had begun on the way out here today—a drive she'd dreaded for the wayward feelings PJ had been evoking ever since she'd walked into his office two days before. And yes, the feelings were there, but as they'd talked during the drive, she'd felt an understanding in him that she'd never experienced with Jon.

Jon was a wonderful, kind, committed man. He had given his life so far to his profession. But he'd sensed something lacking, just as she had. When they'd met at the hospital it had been like finding a kindred spirit.

But not quite as kindred as PJ.

She and Jon wanted the same things, but sometimes she wondered if he really knew who she was. He'd never listened to her the way PJ had today—the way she now remembered that PJ always had.

And while she had tried to know Jon—and his work—better, too, he never shared much of it. Whenever she'd asked, he'd given brief weary answers. "I don't want to talk about it," he often said. "I want to get away from it when I'm with you."

She understood that, but somehow she felt shut out. Sometimes she wondered if Jon thought she was too stupid to understand what he might tell her.

Admittedly maybe she would be. But she wished he would try. It might bring them closer together.

PJ had told her about his windsurfer today. She hadn't understood all of that, either. But he'd made the effort. And simply seeing his eyes light up as he'd talked about the breakthroughs he'd made and when he realized he'd actually made really significant developments was worth every bit she didn't totally comprehend.

She'd felt a growing sense of connection with him on a whole other level than simple sexual awareness.

And then there was the connections she made with his family. *Her* family now, according to his mother.

Of course Ally had told herself that wasn't true, that she had no right to be feeling the sense of welcome and belonging she had felt almost at once. She'd connected with his sister Martha. She'd been delighted with his sister-in-law Tallie and amazed that Tallie had actually baked her cookies to say how happy she was that Ally was part of the family.

It wasn't just that they were marvelous—Tallie, after all, was an accomplished baker who had given up being president of Antonides Marine to become apprentice to a baker in Vienna— it was that she'd made them expressly for Ally.

"I owe you," she'd told Ally frankly. And when Ally had looked at her blankly, Tallie had elaborated, "If you had stayed in Hawaii, I'm sure PJ would never have come back to New York when he did. Which allowed me to shanghai him into taking over for me so I could leave, which meant Elias could go crazy wondering where I was and come halfway round the world to track me down. So in reality, I owe you my husband and my marriage and—" she patted her bulging belly "—my family." She'd positively beamed adding, "That's easily worth a truckload of cookies."

Even PJ's mother had welcomed her. And Helena Antonides would certainly have been within her rights to demand a whole lot more allegiance to her son—not to mention presence—than Ally had ever given PJ. And, ultimately, even his grandmother had, in her way, been kind.

His grandmother had—at least he'd said she had—told him to kiss her.

Ally's face warmed at the thought.

And then there were the babies. Maybe it was seeing all those little Antonides babies that had intensified her feelings. Maybe it was balancing one of Elias and Tallie's twins on each hip and finding herself imagining what it would be like to hold a wriggling little facsimile of PJ. Or maybe it was being handed month-old Liana, the Costanides's only granddaughter, and rocking her to sleep. Or maybe it was seeing PJ do the same thing with his overwrought overtired nephew Edward when no one else could calm him down.

She'd studied a host of paintings of mothers and children in her university art classes, but as far as she was concerned, they were missing the boat by not having one of fathers and children as well.

PJ could model for them all. The look of quiet tenderness on such a masculine face touched her heart. Dear God, he would make beautiful babies. The thought was seriously tempting.

But the truth was, the biggest temptation was PJ himself.

And far from getting him out of her mind by coming to give him the divorce papers in person, she had actually opened a Pandora's box of feelings and needs and connections that she was having an increasingly hard time shoving back in.

And exactly how spending the night in the same bed with PJ was going to shut that box she wasn't sure.

But when she opened the door to the bedroom, she stared around in astonishment.

PJ was gone.

Lukas took one look at her when she came down stairs in the morning and said cheerfully, "Wow. Must've been quite a night."

It was just past eight, but she'd never really slept. Had barely closed her eyes. Half a dozen times during the night she'd told herself she should call Jon. Jon was the one who mattered.

But she hadn't called him. Hadn't even been able to think about him. Had only thought about PJ—about what she'd said to him, about his reaction.

She wished he'd come back, wished she could take the words back, soften them, apologize. And she'd vowed to do so as soon as he reappeared.

But though she lay there waiting, tensing at every sound in the hallway, none of the sounds had been PJ. She'd waited and waited.

He'd never come.

By dawn it was too late to call Jon—and she couldn't have done it then, anyway. It felt all wrong. If it were right, Jon would make the first move and call her.

Not that it mattered. After she had sorted things out with PJ, she would call. She'd brought her phone down with her and set it on the small desk in the kitchen as she tried to muster a bright smile to meet the interested gazes of all of PJ's family.

"Night?" she echoed, not quite sure what he meant.

But his grin made it abundantly clear as he shoveled in another bite of his breakfast. "Both you and PJ look, um, well...not exactly well rested." The grin broadened.

"Lukas!" His mother pointed a spoon at him. "Don't be rude."

"Who me? I'm not rude. Just observant." He shrugged unrepentantly. "And envious."

He certainly had nothing to be envious of, Ally thought grimly.

"Where is PJ?" she said. "I was...in the shower," she explained, hoping it would sound as if that was how she'd missed hearing where he had gone.

"Gone surfing," Lukas said. "How come you didn't go along?"

"I'm sure Ally was still asleep when he left," Helena said. "He likes to be out there early. Sit down. Have some breakfast."

"I'd have stayed in bed," Lukas said with a wink.

His mother thwacked him on the head with her spoon.

"Guess you'll have to find a girl of your own," Martha said unsympathetically. "Got any sisters at home for him?" she asked Ally.

"I'm an only child. I think I'll just go look for PJ," she said to his mother, "instead of eating now." She couldn't have forced down a mouthful anyway. "If you don't mind."

Helena smiled at her. "Not at all. Go right ahead. You two can have breakfast when you come back."

Ally escaped gratefully out onto the deck overlooking the beach and the ocean beyond. The morning air was almost still. The slightest breeze was blowing in off the water as she made her way across the lawn and down the steps to the sand. It was already warm and humid.

Out on the water she could see a lone surfer sitting on his board, drifting, as a set of waves began building behind him. The waves here were nothing like the ones in Hawaii. These were small, tame waves. Not a challenge for PJ, which might have been why he let them slide underneath his board, not paddling to get into position to ride any of them in.

Or maybe it was just that he didn't want to talk to her.

She didn't blame him, she supposed. In her confusion last night, she had created an awkward situation. PJ had gone and he had never come back. And Ally had sat there, huddled and miserable, knowing she had driven him away.

And having done so, rather than feeling relieved that she wouldn't have to share the bed with him, she felt bereft.

Now she sat down on the cool sand beside his towel and, pulling her knees up against her chest, wrapped her arms around them as she watched him.

He had to see her, but he made no move to catch a wave or paddle in. He kept sitting out there, letting his hands dangle in the water, moving them just enough to keep his position, his gaze mostly on the horizon, not on the beach. Not on her.

Another set of waves rolled in, he made a slight move to catch one of them, but didn't, instead letting it roll past.

Ally felt her frustration increasing with every wave he ignored. Finally she stood up and stared out at him. She knew he was looking at her and, she imagined, was pleased that he'd waited her out and that she'd got tired of sitting there expecting him to finally come in.

She kicked off her flip-flops and walked down to the water. She wasn't wearing her bathing suit. But the shorts and T-shirt she did wear were just going to have to get wet.

The water was cool as she waded out. The sea lapped her calves, then her knees, then her thighs. She kept walking. He had stopped glancing back at the swells building behind him now, and was completely focused on her.

She was close enough to see his brows draw down. He sculled with his hands, turning his board toward the shoreline. She was up to her waist now. A wave broke just beyond her, and as it surged past, it soaked her up to the neck.

"What the hell are you doing?" His irritation was obvious.

Ally didn't answer, just dove under the next wave and came up on the other side, far closer to him now. Water streamed down her face. She shook her hair back, wishing she'd thought to put it in a ponytail. But who knew she'd be going swimming?

She pushed off the bottom as the water lapped against her chest and, keeping her gaze fixed on him, began paddling the last ten yards. He watched her come, his hands not drifting in the water any longer. His arms were folded across his chest.

He made no move toward her as she closed the distance between them and grasped the nose of his board.

"What're you doing?" he repeated, sounding annoyed and not at all welcoming. "You're crazy."

"You're chicken," she replied.

He frowned blackly. "I'm chicken?" he echoed her words. "How do you figure?"

"You knew I wanted to talk to you this morning. You wouldn't come in."

"I'm surfing, in case you didn't notice."

"As a matter of fact, I didn't," she said smiling up at him. "Didn't see you catch a wave. Saw a few good ones you ignored."

"They weren't good enough." He looked away, jaw set.

"Ah, what a pity," she said in a light mocking tone. "Waiting for the wave of the day?"

"What difference does it make to you?" There was a hard edge to his voice. He still didn't glance her way.

"PJ," she said, willing him to look at her, waiting until he spared her a bare glance before she said, "I'm sorry."

His gaze jerked back to meet hers. He didn't speak, but he was clearly interested now.

"I apologize," she said sincerely, all flippancy gone. "I shouldn't have said what I did last night. Shouldn't have acted the way I did. It was the way I acted when you came to my opening. I was…chicken then."

He stared at her in disbelief.

"I was," she admitted. "And I was last night, too. Chicken. And confused."

A muscle ticked in his jaw. Then, "You're not the only one," he muttered, and turned to stare out toward the horizon.

Maybe it was better that way. Maybe it would be easier to continue, to explain, if he didn't look at her.

Ally pressed on. "I wanted—" she began, but then she stopped because the truth was she didn't even know exactly what she wanted "—I didn't know what I wanted. I guess the bed situation was the last straw. I don't know what's happening between us," she admitted. "I guess I…wanted to find out."

His head came around and he looked at her again, his expression unreadable. And then he said skeptically, "And you expected to find that out with no kissing?"

"I told you I was confused."

He reached out a hand. "Come here."

For an instant she didn't move, caught by the feeling that she was standing on the edge of a chasm, as if taking that single step of putting her hand in his would be the equivalent of stepping off into space.

But teetering forever on the precipice wasn't an option. And now that she'd come out here, what else was she going to do?

Offer her lame apology, then turn around and swim away?

Or take the hand he offered and find out where they would go from there?

He was waiting, hand still outstretched, his green eyes challenging. He'd made one move. It was up to her to make the other.

Ally lifted her hand and put it in his, felt strong cool fingers wrap around hers. Then almost effortlessly he drew her up out of the water, and the next thing she knew she was able to scramble up onto the board to sit facing him.

"Right," he said hoarsely, letting go of her hand to grasp her by the arms. "Rules be damned." And then he hauled her into his arms and kissed her.

And there it was—that mindless all-consuming longing—all over again.

Every time PJ kissed her she lost her bearings. The sane and sensible Ally vanished and this one went up in flames. The young, earnest, buttoned-down, pent-up Ally—the teenage girl who had always hankered after "the boy with the surfboard" PJ had been—was instantly resurrected by the touch of PJ's lips on hers.

Those demanding persuasive lips made her forget her determination to marry Jon, to be the prodigal daughter come home to make her father happy. They made her forget everything except the man kissing her.

And the taste of him now, mingled with the sea water and warmth of the morning sun brought back to her all her youthful unspoken yearnings, and she thought, *Why not? Why can't I have him? Why can't I love him? He's my husband.*

And the counterbalancing thoughts, *He wants to stay married because it's convenient. He wants me. But he doesn't love me,* were nowhere to be found.

Not that she looked.

She couldn't look, had no brain cells left to look, to think rationally, to do more than kiss him back.

There was only hunger and need and desire—for PJ.

She kissed him openly, eagerly. She let her hands rove over his bare back, relishing the feel of smooth sun-warmed skin under her fingers. She nuzzled her nose against his cheek, and delighted in the scrape of a day's worth of rough whiskers. And if she was enjoying it, reveling in it, there was no question but that the enjoyment was mutual.

PJ bent his head and kissed his way down her neck. Ally instinctively tipped her head back to allow him access. His fingers snaked under her wet T-shirt to splay against her ribs just below her breasts, and his thumbs lifted to caress her, to rub lightly against her nipples, and Ally loved it, arching her back.

"You *would* have to wear a damn T-shirt," he muttered.

She smiled and brushed her fingers lightly against the obviously straining erection beneath the fabric of his shorts. "You would have to wear damn board shorts," she countered.

He gave a pained laugh. "Didn't want to shock my mother when she looked out of her kitchen window. Besides, how did I know you were going to come out here and do this?"

Ally shrugged awkwardly, suddenly self-conscious, yet at the same time oddly liberated. She smiled and looked him in the eyes for a split second. But what she felt for him was too strong, too overwhelming, and she had to look away.

"Hey." His voice was low and almost tender. "Al?" And she felt cool fingers on her cheek, turning her head so she had to look at him or close her eyes. "What's wrong?"

Wrong? "N-nothing." Only that she knew she still loved him. And recognizing it for the truth at last, she was powerless to fight it anymore.

PJ was the man she was in love with, not Jon. He was the man she hungered for, not Jon. He was the man she wanted to spend forever with, and not anyone else at all.

If he read it on her face or saw it in her eyes, she didn't know. She only knew he caught his breath at the same time she caught hers.

"Oh, God," he muttered, and took her mouth again.

His kiss was tender at first, then deeper, more passionate, a simple tasting at first, then eager and devouring as his arms wrapped her and he pulled her close.

Ally wobbled and clung to PJ, pulling herself closer, pressing against him and feeling the press of his body even more insistently against her—wanting, needing—

And then, abruptly, PJ flipped them both into the water!

Ally sputtered to the surface at the same time he did. "What the—"

PJ simply dipped his head toward the beach. And Ally knew the answer even as he said, "You know what."

Yes, indeed she did. In another few moments, without PJ's timely intervention, they would have scandalized his family and undoubtedly broken several laws of the state of New York. Her lack of control appalled her, and her face burned even as her body still continued to simmer.

"Sorry."

PJ gave her a rueful smile. "Me, too. And not because we would have shocked them, either." He reached across the surfboard and grasped her hand, giving it a tight squeeze. "Just—hold that thought."

As if she could do anything else.

They rode the board in together, and it was the first time Ally had surfed in ten years. It was magical—the swoop and the speed of the board on the wave, the excitement and the thrill of the ride and—most of all, the touch of PJ's fingers against her back.

And the audience of Antonides family members who had come down to the beach weren't scandalized at all. They cheered and applauded at the end of the ride as they came out of the water, PJ hoisting the board under one arm while he slung the other over Ally's shoulders.

Yiayia smiled approvingly after they had dried off on the deck and came into the kitchen. She looked up from her rocking chair and nodded and winked at PJ. "A little kissing, *ne?* I told you so."

PJ grinned broadly. "My grandmother is a know-it-all." He bent and gave her a kiss too.

She beamed and sighed with satisfaction. "*Ne*. A grandmother knows."

Wouldn't you know?

He'd suffered through, if not the night from hell—which would have been spending it in bed with Ally without so much as a kiss—at least a very miserable night of purgatory during which he'd walked the beach until dawn.

He should have known better, he'd told himself. He'd pushed it, glibly telling her he was sharing the room—and the bed— with her. He could have handled it differently, not been quite so blithely confrontational, backing her into a corner that way.

But hell's bells, why shouldn't he? he'd thought. She was his wife!

But when she'd simply accepted sleeping with him—in a nonbiblical sense—all the while insisting on "no kissing," he'd stalked out. He had enough control. That wasn't what he was worried about. But he was damned if he was going to lie there chastely beside his wife who didn't want him and was preserving her intimacies for another man.

He'd been furious—and hours of pounding the sand had left him exhausted but no less angry. He'd gone surfing at first light because if anything would calm him and allow him to regain control of his badly frayed composure, it was time alone, just he and his board and the waves.

The ocean was strong, far more powerful than he was, and could be erratic and unpredictable. He didn't control it, but he understood it. He didn't understand Ally.

The time he'd spent in the water had settled him somewhat. He'd had to focus, to get in sync with the waves, to stop thinking about her and what her coming back into his life was making him want. And as time passed, he found his balance again, settled, steadied.

And then he'd spotted her walking toward him on the beach.

The fury had come back, swamping him. And it was all he could do to sit there and ignore her. He'd have preferred paddling to Tierra del Fuego.

She hadn't gone away. She'd stood there waiting. And he'd thought to himself, she could wait till kingdom come. He was damned well not going to catch a wave and ride in to her.

He'd been shocked when she'd swum out to him.

But that had been only half the shock he'd felt when she'd apologized!

What did it mean? He didn't know. And from what she said, she didn't know, either. But there was a light in her eyes now that made him even hungrier for her than he'd been last night. There was an eagerness in her that matched his own.

And of course he could do nothing about it. Not now.

He couldn't haul her off to bed in the middle of the morning. Not with all his family and what seemed like half of the world turning up for one of his mother's legendary brunches.

His father and Elias and Ari Cristopolous wanted him for a foursome on the golf course. PJ was a reluctant golfer at the best of times.

"I don't play," he told his brother, hoping to get out of it.

"It's not play. It's work," Elias replied, then added archly. "Besides, you can't do what you want to do anyway, so you might as well give in gracefully."

PJ shot him a startled look, aware that his ears were reddening. "How do you know what I want to do?" he grumbled.

Elias just shook his head and grinned. "Been there, done that."

PJ doubted it. But he remembered that Elias's courtship had not been exactly smooth, even though it had at least taken place on the right side of the wedding, unlike PJ's own. "All right. Fine."

And it might have been if Ally hadn't decided to come, too. "Only to watch," she said. "Not to play."

But having her right there, sitting next to him in the car, her thigh alongside his, her hair blowing in his face, the scent of her shampoo tantalizing him on the way to the golf course did nothing for his mental preparation. He couldn't even remember which club to use.

"It's called a driver for a reason," Elias pointed out mildly once or twice.

But PJ was oblivious to everyone and everything except Ally. He lost badly. He didn't care. He looked at Ally and smiled, and had won enough when she smiled back at him.

He was eager to get off the course, to get back to the house. To the bedroom. To the bed.

But of course, that didn't happen. When they got back to the house, Mark and Cristina and Alex had arrived. Then Elias and Tallie's friends, the Costanideses, all showed up. So did the Alexakises.

"Why didn't you just invite everybody in Greece?" he grumbled.

His father smiled with beatific unconcern. "We did."

Probably they hadn't. It just seemed like it. And there was nothing he could do but smile at them, talk to them, introduce them to Ally.

He made sure he introduced them to Ally. And they were all as charmed as he was.

Cristina wanted to haul her off to the sewing room to talk art. Martha was eager to continue yesterday's conversation. It turned out that Connie Cristopolous was a mosaic artist as well. They were all eager to chat.

"Another time," PJ said gruffly. He had his fingers manacled around Ally's wrist and he wasn't letting go. He was afraid of what might happen, of a possible change in heart, if he let her out of his sight.

"You could come, too," Ally suggested, eyes twinkling.

"Nah. I'd rather play with the kids on the beach." He looked at her. "Wouldn't you?"

He'd have let her go. Really, he would have. And he might

even have gone with her if that was what she really wanted. But his spirits soared even higher when she smiled and nodded. "Yes. We can talk about this later," she said to Cristina and Connie and Martha. "Let's play with the kids."

They played with the kids. Besides the nephews, there were several little Costanides boys and the Alexakises had a boy and three girls. There were others, too, belonging to cousins and friends of his parents.

PJ couldn't keep them all straight and didn't try. What he noticed was Ally. The Ally he remembered had always been quiet, almost inhibited, a girl who rarely let go and played. But this Ally came alive with the children in a way he'd never seen before.

She got totally involved in building a sand castle with the little kids. And when he and Lukas and some of the bigger boys splashed them playfully with water—which of course turned into a water fight—she took great joy in dousing him. She was also the one who suggested "burying Uncle PJ in the sand" would be a grand game.

"Whoa, hang on," he'd protested.

But to no avail. Not when Elias and Lukas and even his mother agreed and helped dig the hole. At least she'd dug him out after and spent an inordinate amount of time brushing sand off him.

He'd loved every minute of that. Too much, in fact, and he'd finally had to head straight into the ocean before he scandalized his entire family.

When he came back it was to discover she had yet another idea—they should make face paint.

He stared at her. "Face paint?"

She grinned impishly. "Chicken?"

"Of course not," he said, affronted. "But how…?" Face paint was totally out of his area of expertise.

"We'll be right back," she promised the kids and, grabbing him by the hand, she led him into the house.

It was not the mystery he imagined it would be—not the mystery that Ally herself was. Cornstarch, cold cream, a few drops of water and food coloring and they were in business. He regarded the colorful tubs a bit warily.

Ally giggled. "Here," and in an instant she dabbed his nose with blob of green. "How handsome you are."

"Am I?" PJ growled and, dipping his fingers in the blue, set off after her while she dodged away, laughing, nearly colliding with his mother and falling over *Yiayia* in her rocking chair.

"Out!" His mother flapped her hands at both of them, shaking her head as well. "You're terrible! Who'd have thought PJ would marry a woman as crazy as he is?"

Ally stopped dead, looking stricken, all laughter gone. "Am I?"

"As crazy as he is?" PJ's mother looked surprised at how serious Ally seemed. Then, as if realizing Ally needed reassurance, she smiled and gave her daughter-in-law a hug. "Yes, I think you are." Then she stroked a motherly hand over Ally's silken midnight hair. "But that's a good thing, you understand?"

Ally looked from his mother to PJ himself, and he saw that her eyes were wide with something that looked like wonder. Then she smiled with a joy PJ had rarely seen as she gave his mother a hard hug in return. "Thank you. Thank you so much."

PJ, watching them, felt for the first time that the tide might really actually have turned. "Ally?"

She looked his way, eyes still glowing.

Grinning, he reached out a hand and stroked blue face paint across her cheeks.

CHAPTER NINE

TONIGHT she was going to make love with PJ Antonides.

She'd been waiting for it all day.

No, not really waiting, because that seemed somehow to imply that she'd done nothing else. And she'd done a lot, enjoyed a lot.

It had been a magical day.

Not a day. The whole weekend had been magical. In all of it—with the exception of the horrible sleepless night she'd spent last night which was, let's face it, her own fault—Ally had discovered the happiest two days of her life.

The weekend she'd faced with trepidation and anxiety had turned into one of joy and good feeling. With their easy smiles and eager embrace, PJ's family had given her the warmth and sense of belonging she'd always wanted. Completely unexpectedly, under distinctly dubious circumstances, they had opened their arms to her, taken her in, made her their own.

And PJ?

She was about to let him make her his own as well.

She wasn't standing on the precipice any longer, torn between the man she'd conveniently and desperately married and the future she'd envisioned with Jon.

On the contrary, with her apology, she'd taken a step, made a move. And she was free-falling now, inexorably pulled by the attraction she'd felt from the first time she'd met PJ Antonides, an attraction that, unbelievably, hadn't diminished over the past ten years.

But it was more than simple physical attraction. And it was more than the camaraderie of old friendship renewed.

She was very much afraid it was love. Real love. A love that had begun all those years ago and had endured despite their separation, and that had only needed proximity to rekindle, to spark to life again.

At least, it was doing so for her.

She still didn't know how PJ felt. She knew he wanted to continue their marriage—for the moment at least. He'd made that much clear.

But it was also clear that being married was convenient for him. And he'd offered no declarations of love. In fact, he'd agreed that day in his office that he couldn't possibly love her.

And yet...

She hoped. She remembered the way he looked at her sometimes...the way he touched her...the way he'd kissed...

And so she had to find out.

What she'd had with PJ that single night ten years ago—and what they'd shared so far this weekend—both felt so different, so much more authentic than what she'd determinedly tried to construct with Jon, that she couldn't just turn her back and walk away.

And so when, at long last, night fell and the party broke up and PJ came with her to their bedroom, she didn't demur, she didn't act coy, she didn't protest. On the contrary, this time she was the one who grasped his wrist and drew him in with her, then shut the door.

One of PJ's dark brows lifted quizzically. His eyes were dark and heavy-lidded now, slumberous almost. Bedroom eyes. It was an expression Ally had never understood before. Now she did—and didn't need an explanation, either. She had only to look at the man whose lips were scant inches from her own, whose breath she could feel against her heated skin, whose lips she wanted to taste.

She drew an anticipatory breath, then ran her tongue over her own lips.

PJ groaned.

"What's wrong?" she demanded. "Are you sick?" With the amount of food his mother and grandmother and aunts had been making and PJ and his brothers had been eating, she wouldn't have been surprised.

But he was smiling as he shook his head. "Not unless you say 'No kissing.' You're not gonna say that, are you?"

And then she smiled, too, and went up on her toes to brush her mouth against his. "What do you think?"

His lips curved against her own, the merest yet most tantalizing graze of flesh against flesh. His words seemed to vibrate through her as he murmured, "I think that's an even better idea than the face paint, Mrs. Antonides."

And then he took over. His mouth closed over hers, softly at first, gently almost, but with a hunger that built quickly because she had been waiting for it, hoping for it, all day. Maybe, in fact, she'd been waiting for it since their wedding night. The brief quick hungry kisses they'd shared in the past few days were mere appetizers in the face of the feast that PJ was making of this.

It was definitely a kiss worth waiting for.

Ally forgot all about her worries, her nerves, her confusion. She could only respond to the sweet persuasiveness of his lips, his tongue, could only open to him, welcome him, meet his hunger with her own.

But even though he was clearly as desperate for it as she was, his kiss was deliberately slow and leisurely, as if he was a man about to partake of a feast and for whom slow meticulous preparation was every bit as important as the meal he was about to enjoy.

And Ally enjoyed it, too.

She relished the taste of him, all salt and sea spray with, somehow, a hint of lime. In his hair she caught the scent of wood smoke from the evening fire. She drew it in, savored it, even as she savored the silky softness of it threading through her fingers. Then she turned her face to enjoy the scrape of rough whiskers against the softness of her cheek.

He slid his hands up under her shirt, then tugged it effortlessly over her head. The night air through the open window cooled her own heated flesh, but didn't cool her ardor. She snagged the hem of his T-shirt and pulled it up and over his head.

"Mmm." He murmured and backed her toward the bed.

It was the bed in which she'd lain sleepless virtually all night, last night. It was the bed that had seemed as vast and cold as an arctic wasteland when she had spent hours in it alone. But tonight, as PJ bore her back down on it, it seemed a warm and welcome cocoon for the two of them to share.

"Do you want to leave the light on?" he asked. "Or off?"

She hesitated. A part of her would prefer to leave it on, to see PJ strip off and bare the splendor of his naked body. A part of her imagined that he would enjoy the same view of her.

Maybe it was self-consciousness that had her whisper, "Off?" almost as if it were a question. Or self-preservation. Or maybe it was an almost unconscious desire to re-create the intimacy of their wedding night. Then they had embraced in the darkness with only the rising moon to light the room.

Now as PJ flicked off the lamp, she found that there was indeed the same soft silver of moonglow bathing the room. She just prayed that this time the love they shared would last beyond the dawn.

If PJ had similar memories, he didn't say. He didn't speak at all. His hands, his lips, his body spoke for him. He pressed her back onto the bed and made slow sweet love to her.

His touches made her quiver with longing. His fingers trailing down over her ribs and then up the length of her legs made her bite her lip with frustration. But at the same time, she gave herself over to enjoying their touch, reveling in the fact that she was in PJ's arms, in his bed, where she'd never imagined being again.

And then his fingers finally found her, touching her where she most needed his touch, stroking her, opening her. And she sucked in a sharp breath at the sweetness of it, even as she twisted on the sheets and reached out to touch him as well.

Very quickly the rest of their clothes slipped away—and for a second she regretted not having more light to see him. But sight wasn't the only sense she had. Even in the near darkness she could feel his firmly muscled body, his heated flesh, his hair-roughened skin. She could trail her fingers down his abdomen, could run a single one along the proud jut of his erection, making him tense and shudder.

"Ally!" He groaned her name.

She smiled and pressed kisses into his chest, his belly, his—

"Ally!" He hauled her up and pressed her into the sheets. "You're going to kill me, doing that."

"Oh, I wouldn't want to kill you," she whispered. "I have a much better idea." And she wrapped her hands across his back pulling him closer so that their bodies fit together completely.

His knee nudged between hers and she shifted to accommodate. It had been so long, and yet in another way it felt as if no time had passed, as if the memories of that night melded into this one, just as their separate movements meshed and melded into one, as if her body knew what she had not known—that she was his and always had been.

He moved against her, pressed in, and she wrapped her legs around him, her fingers digging into his back as they rocked together, eager, hungry, desperate as the sensation built.

It was like catching a wave, feeling the surging power of the ocean as it lifted them, then plunged them over the crest to ride together, spent yet exhilarated, to shore.

It was like last time, and yet, as the moon slipped slowly across the sky and they loved and touched and stroked and murmured—and kissed and kissed and kissed—Ally knew that this night promised more than the first night. There was eagerness, yes. But the urgency of the moment in their earlier love-making—the grasping of a single night out of time—was no longer there.

This was different, Ally thought after they had taken each other a second time and lay tangled together in joyful exhaustion. This wasn't a single moment or even a single night.

It was the beginning of a lifetime together.

Or if it wasn't, if she was wrong, this night would have to last her a lifetime.

Even though PJ didn't speak, didn't offer her endearments, she didn't care. Words didn't mean that much. It was what you showed each other, what your actions said to each other, what you gave that really spoke of how you felt.

And the truth was, PJ had given her years of his life. He'd given her time to grow up, to become a woman he could meet as an equal, be proud of and, she hoped, come to love.

And Ally was determined to, desperately wanted to, be worthy of that love—and to give the same to him. She knew what she wanted now—just as she finally understood what she had to give.

This time she didn't need to turn her back on PJ to go away to find herself. This time she needed to stay, to give herself—to take up her marriage again and make it work.

Tonight he'd made love with Ally Maruyama. No, with Ally Antonides.

He'd waited all day for it.

No, not all day. Ten years.

He lay there now in the room he'd grown up in, where he'd planned his wild adventures and dreamed his impossible dreams, and knew that the boy he'd been could never have dreamed or planned this.

He lay with his arms wrapped securely, possessively, protectively around his wife. Ally's head rested on his chest, her hair tickling his nose. She was sound asleep, breathing softly. Satisfied and sated, he hoped.

Heaven knew he was. For the moment, at least. But probably not for long. He had ten years of loving to make up for. Ten years of doing without.

He hadn't thought about it that way before. He hadn't known, of course. He'd been young and raw and blind when they'd married. He hadn't thought, hadn't considered the consequences, had only acted on his instincts.

And his instincts, come to think of it, hadn't been bad at all.

But he'd never really thought beyond the night. Even when spending it with her had caused him to catch a glimmer of what actually loving a woman like Ally might mean, he'd known it wouldn't work.

She hadn't asked for that. And neither had he.

So he'd given her what she wanted—his name on a legal document and one night in his bed, in his arms.

That was then.

At thirty-two he was a different man. Wiser, he hoped. Steadier. A whole hell of a lot more responsible. And he was no longer interested in living solely for the moment. He wanted a future as well. He was grown up now. A man, with a man's knowledge of time and sense of missed opportunities, of waves not caught, of loves lost.

Well, he wasn't losing this time, he thought, stroking her hair, and smiling when she stirred and her fingers moved against him.

"Again?" she asked with a sleepy smile. Her fingers found him, stroked him.

He arched. "Ally," he warned because amazingly enough he was ready again.

"PJ," she acknowledged. And she turned her head and kissed his chest, licked his nipple.

His breath hissed, and he pulled her on top of him, settling her over him, thrusting up to meet her, closing his eyes as she took him in. Then they opened again so he could watch her the silver of the moonlight, could relish the shadowy mo and curves, the silken curtain of her hair. He lifted his hands and cupped her breasts, shaped them, learned them all over again.

She pressed down on him, then rose and slid down again, making him clench his teeth at the feel of her body taking him in. She sighed and her head dropped back exposing the delicate curve of her neck. He longed to kiss it.

"Ally." He urged her down so he could. And did.

Their bodies rocked together. Found a rhythm.

Wasn't going to lose her this time. Wasn't going to let her walk away. Not too late. It wasn't too late.

The words echoed in his ears faster and more frantically as the rhythm quickened, as the need built. Then, as once more the climax came, PJ clenched his teeth and pulled her down to hold her tight against him.

This time he had to make her want to stay—not just for a night, but for a lifetime.

This time he was giving it all he had.

The tapping sound woke her.

Ally was tangled amongst sheets and blankets and PJ, her face in the curve of his neck, his arm flung over her, her knee captured between his.

It was awkward and ache-making and absolutely wonderful—just as the whole night had been. Better even than their wedding night because he was still here and—

The tapping came again. Louder now. More emphatic. Someone was knocking on the bedroom door.

One of the kids, no doubt. She'd heard them up and about yesterday, the patter—and thud—of small feet up and down the hallway while she'd lain here alone and miserable. Yesterday morning they wouldn't have considered awakening her. They ̲ ̲ ̲ ̲ wn her. But she and PJ had become serious favor- ̲ ̲ ̲ ̲ ounger set by dinnertime.

̲ ̲ ̲ wasn't the only thing that had changed.

̲ ̲ ̲ ed her head and laid a gentle kiss on the whisker-roughened jaw of the man who had changed them. He didn't stir, but then, he had to be exhausted.

The tapping came again. Harder. More brisk. "PJ? Ally?"

Not one of the kids, then. In fact the voice sounded like Elias or Lukas. It also sounded urgent.

Ally eased her way out of PJ's embrace, not wanting to wake him if she didn't have to. She knew exactly how little sleep he'd got last night—and he probably hadn't had much more the night before.

She tugged her nightshirt over her head, grabbed her robe and pulled it on, threw a sheet over the most exposed bits of PJ, then padded over to open the door a few inches and peer into Elias's face.

"Oh, God," he said. "I'd hoped it would be PJ."

Ally frowned. "What's wrong?"

Something clearly was. His normally tanned face was uncharacteristically pale. A muscle in his jaw seemed to tick.

"I wanted to tell him, then he could have told you."

Ally's heart suddenly bumped. "Tell me what?"

"Someone named Jon called."

He paused just long enough for Ally to find herself thinking ironically, Jon *never* calls. *Why now?*

And then Elias told her. "Your father's had a heart attack."

CHAPTER TEN

"I SHOULD have called!" Ally was whirling around the room throwing things in her suitcase, her cheeks flushed, her hair flying.

"Called? Called who?" PJ wasn't even awake yet. How the hell could he be? He'd been awake most of the night. The wonderful lovely night. The absolutely fabulous spectacular night. The best night of his life—

And now Ally had turned into a whirling dervish. He rolled over and shoved himself up, still foggy with sleep or lack thereof, and tried to figure out what the hell was going on. His gaze, following her from the closet to the suitcase, passed the doorway. His head jerked. He squinted. *"Elias?* What the hell—"

Elias came in and shut the door, leaning against it. *"Yiayia* answered her phone," he explained, plucking it from his pocket.

Ally stopped tossing things in her suitcase and snatched it from his hand, then began to punch in numbers.

"Ally's dad had a heart attack," Elias went on.

PJ sat up straight, appalled, his gaze on Ally. Her movements were almost frantic.

"He's alive," Elias said. "But only just, apparently. *Yiayia* didn't know more than that. She grabbed me and told me to tell Ally."

PJ had a thousand questions. The only one that seemed likely to be answered was, What the hell was *Yiayia* doing with Ally's phone?"

It didn't make sense. None of it.

He wanted to shut it off and go back to sleep, to dream the dreams he'd been dreaming, to relive the night he and Ally had shared—a night that, from the look of her hunched shoulders and nervously tapping toes, she probably didn't even remember.

"She left her phone in the kitchen. It rang." Elias shrugged helplessly. "*Yiayia* answered it."

"Ally's phone?"

Elias spread his hands. "*Yiayia* has no concept of cell phones. Or messaging. She thinks that if a phone rings, you answer it. Sorry," he said to Ally.

But Ally wasn't listening. She was pacing and breathing rapidly, alternately biting her lip, clenching her fist and hugging herself with one arm across her chest. "Answer the phone, damn it!" she exclaimed. "Jon, I'm here. Call back for God's sake and tell me what's happening? And tell Dad I'm on my way!"

Then she flicked it off and continued to fling her clothes into the suitcase.

"Beat it," PJ said to his brother. Then added a gruff, "Thanks," as Elias nodded and opened the door.

"Don't thank me," Elias said over his shoulder. "This is nothing to be thankful for."

And wasn't that the truth?

As soon as his brother left, PJ got out of bed. Ally was stabbing at the phone again, then flinging it down in disgust.

"I should have called," she wailed. "I shouldn't have left him."

"Your being there wouldn't have stopped him having a heart attack," PJ said reasonably.

But Ally was pretty much beyond reason. She shook her head. "I shouldn't have left! I should never have come here. I should at least have called! I didn't...I...I have to go home. Now." She looked at him, eyes flashing, a frantic look in them that he'd never seen before, along with a desperation that seemed to dare him to try to stop her.

But PJ had no intention of stopping her.

On the contrary, he was going with her.

He'd let her go to her father by herself the first time—the day they were wed—to inform him of their marriage. She'd said she didn't need him there, that it wasn't his problem, that she could handle it, and he'd believed her.

This time he wasn't even giving her a chance. He had too much at stake now—his life, his future, the woman he loved.

The word snuck up on him. *Love.*

Not lust. Not physical satisfaction. Not simply "making love with" though they'd certainly done that often enough last night. No, this was greater than that, far deeper, far more demanding.

It was the love he'd glimpsed all those years ago—the potential for a relationship that had not only a physical component, but emotional, intellectual and even spiritual dimensions.

It was what he felt for Ally. He knew it. He accepted it. He *wanted* it.

And he wasn't letting her walk away again.

"I'll take care of it," he said, and he wrapped his arms around her and gave her a fierce hard hug.

And then he set about doing exactly that.

Ally felt sick. Desperate. Guilty.

It was true, what she'd told PJ. She should have called. She shouldn't have come. Not to his parents'. Not to New York at all.

She should have left well enough alone, sent the divorce papers, stayed with her father.

Except...except that then she wouldn't have PJ back in her life. She wouldn't have had this past weekend. She wouldn't have had last night.

Could she regret that?

Could she *really?* No, she couldn't.

Guilt and desperation and worry and anguish began bubbling up all over again.

She tried Jon's mobile over and over. She got the same terse businesslike response she got whenever something else in his life took precedence and was too important to permit him to talk to her. Ordinarily she just tried again, didn't take it personally. Of course he was busy.

But her father had had a heart attack! What could possibly be more important than that?

"Call the hospital," PJ suggested. He was using his own phone, making calls, other calls. His own business obviously took precedence, too.

No, that wasn't fair. He'd hugged her. She'd felt his hard arms come around her to hold her close and, for just a second, she'd allowed herself to sag into his strength, to let him hold her, support her. She'd even nodded her head when he'd said he'd take care of it.

But of course he couldn't. How could he take care of her father? She needed to get home.

"I have to call the airline."

"I called. The flight leaves at one." He glanced at his watch. "We've got to get on the road soon. Call the hospital. At least you can find out how he is."

"Yes." But finding out might make it worse. Her fingers fumbled with the address book on her phone. She'd put the number in there when he'd had his first heart attack, used to know it by heart. But her heart was pounding now and her mind was numb and she couldn't even remember how to bring it up.

"Here." PJ took her phone from her. "What's the name of the hospital?"

At least she could remember that.

He got the number in a matter of seconds, and she could hear it ringing through. He handed her the phone just as it was answered.

She gave her father's name in a tremulous voice, afraid he wouldn't be there. Afraid she'd already lost him, afraid it was too late.

But the receptionist said, "Yes. Cardiac intensive care. I'll put you through."

Her legs almost buckled with relief. She gave PJ a tremulous smile. He watched her gravely, his hand on her arm.

She hoped one of the nurses she'd got to know during her father's last heart attack might be on duty now, might remember her, be willing to give her an update.

Where were they? Why didn't they come to the phone? Her shoulders hunched, her fingers tightened. And then she felt PJ's hands on her back, his thumbs pressing, kneading, easing the knotted muscles there. She almost whimpered it felt so good.

And then she heard the click of connection and a voice said, "Alice? Is that you?"

"Jon!"

The hands on her shoulders stilled. She barely noticed. "How is he? He's not—" She couldn't say the words.

Jon heard them, anyway. "Of course he isn't," he said soothingly. "He wouldn't be here if he were, would he? Where have you been? I rang for over an hour."

She certainly couldn't answer that. Not now. "I—it's barely dawn here."

"You should keep your phone on."

"It was. It—I didn't hear it. Just tell me how he is."

"He's had a heart attack, Alice. It's serious. He's resting now and he's conscious, but I don't have to tell you that after his last one, there is cause for concern." Then he went into doctor mode and rattled off a bunch of medical terms and analyses that left Ally realizing maybe she really was too stupid to understand when Jon talked about his work.

But then the medical analysis ended and Jon said, "He thought you'd call. He expected to hear from you."

"I never said—"

"I know. But I thought—well, even *I* expected you'd keep in touch."

"I know. I...meant to. I got sidetracked. I'm sorry." Guilt swamped her again, drowning the small thought that they had phones, too. Jon could have kept in touch, called her. So could her father.

"Never mind. We're still assessing the damage. The first twenty-four hours is critical of course. Medically there is nothing to say this is true, but I imagine he'd do better with you here."

"Of course. I'm on my way. My plane leaves at—" She looked helplessly around for the answer, for PJ.

His fingers squeezed her shoulders. "The flight leaves a little after one," he said, and she remembered that he'd already told her that. She repeated it for Jon.

"So you won't be here until at least eight. I don't know where I'll be, Ally. Maybe you could get a cab from the airport."

"Of course." She knew he wouldn't have time to come and get her. "I'd like— Can I—" But she knew better than to ask to speak to her father. "Just tell him I love him," she said urgently. "And tell him I'm on my way."

"I will."

"And...and I'm sorry, Jon. I'll see you as soon as I can," she said. "I—" she'd been going to say, *I love you.* It had become a virtually automatic end to all her conversations with Jon. But the words stuck in her throat.

There was a pause. Then Jon said, "I have to go. I need to check on your father. I'll see you tonight."

There was a click, and Ally stood there, motionless, gutted, feeling as if, were she to move, she would shatter into a million tiny pieces. She could barely even breathe.

And then she felt the rhythmic magic of PJ's hands on her shoulders again. She felt his breath on her neck. His lips touched her in silent acknowledgment. He was so close she could feel the warmth emanating off his body. And she desperately wanted to lean into it, to let him embrace her, to take away her pain.

But she had caused her own pain. And if she hadn't caused

her father's, she soon would when she told him what she had to tell him when she got home.

"Come on," PJ said after a moment, and he took the phone out of her nerveless fingers with one hand and caught her wrist in the other. "Let's get the stuff into the car."

PJ's parents, his siblings, his whole family were instantly and completely sympathetic. They hovered, they patted, they hugged. His mother and grandmother plied her with food she couldn't eat. His sisters suggested milk and juice and homeopathic tranquilizers.

His father snorted at that and offered her a shot of ouzo to calm her nerves instead.

"She'll throw up, Dad," PJ said firmly.

It was probably the truth.

Ally tried to be polite, to thank them for their concern at the same time she tried to keep a stiff upper lip and maintain some slight version of her father's vaunted Maruyama control.

But, as she feared, she wasn't a very good Maruyama. Her lips quivered when she said, no, thank you, and tears welled when she shook her head. She might have made it with her dignity intact if, just as she was going to get into the car, PJ's grandmother hadn't said, "Wait!" and trundled down the steps to wrap her in her arms and hug her tightly.

And Ally couldn't help but hug her back. It was like hugging her own grandmother, the same small bones, the same tender look, the same fierce love. It undid her completely, and then she couldn't stop the tears that streamed down her face.

"I'm sorry," she murmured. "I'm sorry. I don't mean to."

"*Ne, ne.* It is good that you cry," *Yiayia* said, patting her back, touching her cheek. "You love him."

"I do, yes. But—" But that was only part of why she was crying. There was no way she could explain the guilt she felt. She shook her head and wiped her eyes. "Thank you," she whispered. "For everything."

Yiayia nodded, smiling gently as she touched a finger to Ally's chin. "It will be all right, you see. And when you come back, you bring your papa, *ne?*"

The idea was as preposterous and it was tempting. Mostly it provided Ally with a glimmer of hope. She swallowed and managed a tiny tremulous smile of her own. "I hope so," she said. "Oh, I do hope so."

"It will be all right." PJ tried again to get through to her, break down the wall of reserve Ally had barricaded herself behind.

She didn't answer, just sat there in the car silent as a stone. Every now and then he heard her gulp or sigh or sniffle. But she said barely a word.

"He might be sitting up eating dinner by the time you get there," he persisted, patting her knee in an awkward attempt at consolation. How did you console someone who wouldn't be consoled?

"No," she said tonelessly.

"Ally, listen to me. You always used to tell me what a tough old buzzard he was. How can you possibly think he's going to pop off without a fight?"

She swallowed convulsively and shook her head. "I don't know. He's been fighting—" Her voice broke.

"I thought he wanted to see a grandchild," PJ said firmly. "You don't think he'd stick around for that?"

Tears spilled down her cheeks then and she didn't reply at all.

He knew she was crying for her father. But he suspected there was a lot more to it than that. Guilt, for one thing. A bit desperately he said, "Look, get it through your head, this is not your fault!"

But Ally didn't reply. And if she believed him, he couldn't have said.

All the rest of the way to the airport, she sat with her lips pressed together, staring out the window. He didn't know what she was seeing, but he was pretty sure it wasn't Long Island potato fields or suburban housing tracts. He wanted to reach her, to comfort her, to support her, but she'd created a wall between them and he didn't know the way over.

She didn't speak until they got to the airport and he turned at the long-term parking sign.

Then she roused herself to ask, "What are you doing? It'll be so much faster if you just put me off at the terminal."

"But I'd have to catch up," he said, pulling into the stall and shutting off the engine. "And the plane won't leave any sooner. Come on." He opened the door and got out.

Ally got out, too, and stared as he opened the back and took out their suitcases. Her eyes widened as she pointed to the extra one. "What's that?"

"Mine. I'm coming, too."

She stared, then shook her head as if she didn't believe it. Then shook it again more rapidly as if she did and didn't want to. "No! You can't. I mean, you don't need to do that."

"I want to do it. I'm going to do it."

"But—it's Hawaii! It's hours away!"

"Eleven until we get there," he said, picking up the cases and leading the way to where they could make a transfer. "No big deal."

She kept pace with him, though she nearly had to run to do so. "Really, PJ, it's not necessary!"

But he didn't believe that. Not anymore. He wasn't going to argue about it though. He just shrugged. "Yes it is. And I've got a ticket. I'm coming."

She called the hospital before they boarded the plane. Her father was stable, the nurse said.

"As well as can be expected," Ally reported when PJ asked. "Whatever that means," she muttered.

"It means he's hanging in there," PJ said. He squeezed her icy hand.

She gripped his, too, so tightly it was almost painful. He

didn't care. If he could take her pain, he would. Anything he could do, he would.

He leaned across the armrest between them and planted a kiss on her temple. "You've got to hang in there, too, Ally."

She drew a slow breath, carefully, almost warily, and nodded her head. "Yes."

If there was an unexpected blessing to their having spent most of the past two nights sleepless, the first in misery and the last in each other's arms, it was that eleven hours of forced in-activity meant they had a chance to sleep.

Ally did, eventually. In fits and bits, a couple of hours into the flight. PJ couldn't close his eyes. To do so felt almost like falling asleep on duty. She was his to care for and protect. And so he tucked a blanket around her, sat next to her and kept watch.

She woke once and found him looking at her and said, "I can't believe you're doing this."

"Believe it."

"You have a life."

"I have a wife," he countered.

As far as he was concerned, that was the bottom line.

Ally smiled faintly, almost sadly. And then she closed her eyes again and slept.

If Ally had ever needed a demonstration of the expression "He's got your back" she had it today. PJ had been behind her or beside her—stalwart, strong and steadying—every step of the way.

He'd packed their bags, got their tickets, taken her to the airport, held her hand every inch of the way. He'd let her sleep on his shoulder and wipe her nose on his handkerchief. He'd got a rental car while she'd tried futilely to call Jon, and then he had driven her straight to the hospital. This was Honolulu. He knew his way around.

She was grateful for it. She loved him for it.

The truth was she loved him, period.

He slowed to turn into the hospital parking lot.

"No," she said, "Just drop me at the front entrance. It will be quicker."

He nodded. "Okay. I'll meet you inside. Wait and—"

"No," she said quickly, needing to get it over with. "I have to go by myself."

"No! Last time you went by yourself."

Last time? "You mean—"

"When we got married, you told him on your own. I'm not letting you deal with that this time."

"I have to. You can't come."

He jammed on the brakes and stared at her. "Why?"

She glanced away, unable to take the hurt in his eyes.

"It's not that I don't want you there," she tried to explain. "It's just…he doesn't know. About you, I mean. And me. He thinks Jon— He expects Jon…" She couldn't finish. She could see she didn't have to.

His jaw tightened. His lips pressed into a thin line. "You're saying it will kill him."

"I don't…know." Her voice wobbled. "But I can't take the chance. I can't tell him now. I just need a little time. He'll come around. I know he will. He'll want to meet you…"

But they both knew it wasn't true. The last person in the world her father would want to meet was PJ, the man he blamed for the loss of his daughter for all those years. And now PJ was the fly in the ointment again. He was the man who had given her the chance to leave once before, and now he was the one who stood between her and Jon…

"We'll talk about it later. Promise. I won't be long," she said. "They never let anyone stay long. I'll see him now, talk to Jon. Half an hour. Please?"

His fingers flexed on the steering wheel, knuckles whitening. A muscle in his jaw ticked.

She put her hand on his arm. "I don't want him to die, PJ. I don't want to be the *reason* he dies."

His jaw tightened. "I know that." He let out a harsh breath and stopped the car in front of the hospital entrance. "Go on then."

Ally climbed out, then turned back. "You don't have to stay in the car. You can wait in the lobby. Or come to the cardiac floor. There's a waiting room there. He won't know. All right?"

"I'll park the car."

She leaned across the seat and gave him a quick hard kiss. "Thank you, PJ. You're the best." Then she turned and hurried through the doors.

She'd said that to him on their wedding day, too.

They'd said their vows, had become man and wife and, coming out of the courthouse she taken his arm and looked up into his eyes, a smile bright on her face and she'd said, "Thank you, PJ. You're the best."

He wondered if she even remembered that now.

Certainly she didn't at the moment. At the moment, understandably, she was only thinking about her dad.

He couldn't blame her. If his own dad were in intensive care, he'd be doing whatever needed to be done to make sure the old windbag stayed alive. He loved his unpredictable flamboyant father even when the old man complicated his life. And he didn't doubt that however difficult Ally's father had made her life over the years, she loved him, too.

He could even understand why she didn't want him to come in and meet her father now, though it rankled. No, more than rankled, it hurt.

He'd never even met the man. His father-in-law!

PJ parked the car and pocketed the keys, jingling them in his fingers, weighing his options. But he didn't weigh them for long. He hadn't come all this distance to be turned away at the door.

Ally was his wife, damn it, and he loved her. He wasn't going to interfere, wasn't going to cause problems or upset her or her father. But if Ally needed him, he was going to be there, a heartbeat away.

He turned and headed for the hospital doors.

He'd been in a couple of emergency rooms during his time here before. He'd split his head on a rock one summer, had run a drill bit through his thumb one fall. He'd never had a heart attack, though, so this part was all new to him.

It was less nitty-gritty than the emergency rooms and far more high-tech. Nurses moved with quick efficiency, barely sparing him a glance. He asked for Mr. Maruyama's room.

"Number four," a nurse said, barely glancing up from her charting. "But you can't go in. Only family allowed."

He could have argued. He *was* family. But that would only make things worse.

Besides, he could see the family—Ally—from here.

It wasn't far down the hall and the wall of the room was half glass. The privacy curtains were open.

Ally was standing next to the bed, one of her hands clasped in her father's, the other gently stroking his thinning gray hair. The pinched worried look he'd seen on her face ever since he'd awakened to Elias's news this morning had softened.

But she'd got here in time. And now as she smiled at something her father murmured, a gentle joy seemed to light her face.

A man in a white coat brushed past him, bumping his elbow. "Sorry." But he didn't even glance around, just headed straight toward Ally's father's room.

And as PJ watched, the man swept into the room and wrapped Ally in a hard fierce hug. Her father's gray face seemed almost to light up at the sight of him.

Jon.

PJ didn't move. Just stared.

He could hear nothing they said. He didn't need to. He saw Jon take charge, his manner easy and efficient, his expression concerned as he talked to Mr. Maruyama, but softening with a smile whenever he looked at Ally. PJ's guts twisted.

He saw the old man beam as he looked at the two of them. He reached out a hand and took one of Ally's, then extended it feebly in Jon's direction.

Ally hesitated only for a moment, then, as Jon's hand came out to meet it, let his fingers curl around hers.

"How's that for a happy ending?" The charting nurse smiled up at PJ and put her pen away.

PJ had no words.

He wanted to stalk into the room and rip their hands apart. He wanted to wipe the smile off Jon's cheerful face and the satisfaction off Ally's father's. He wanted to say, "She's mine, damn it! She's my wife. She belongs to me. I love her!"

But it was love, God help him, that stopped him.

Love—not the physical bit, not the touches and caresses and ecstasies they'd shared last night—but the deeper stuff, the harder stuff, the selfless stuff held him right where he was, on the outside, looking in.

Love, real love—"grown-up love" as his sister Cristina had called it just the other day—wasn't about what you wanted. It wasn't about that at all.

And loving Ally wasn't about possessing her, or even about protecting her or giving her such a good time in bed that she couldn't say no to him.

It was wanting what was best for her. Deep down. Gut level. Heart-and-soul level.

It wasn't killing her father's hopes and dreams to make his own come true. PJ knew Ally well enough to know the guilt would destroy her. It would also destroy the very love they shared.

His throat was tight. It hurt to swallow. His jaw was clamped so tight his teeth hurt.

The nurse laid a hand on his arm. "Are you all right? Do you want to go sit down? I'm sure Dr. Tanaka or Mr. Maruyama's daughter will come out and talk to you soon. I can tell them you're here."

Numbly PJ shook his head. "No," he said, his voice rusty with pain. "I have to go."

But still he didn't move, just had to look, to memorize, to hold forever in his heart.

And then Ally looked up and saw him. Her eyes widened. Her whole body tensed.

Of course it did. Because if he walked in there, he would destroy everything she loved.

He drank her in—her soft mouth, her flawless skin, her midnight hair and her wondrous eyes. He closed his own for just a moment, held the vision tight, as if imprinting it on his soul. And then he opened them and gave her back the sad smile she'd given him on the airplane.

He understood it now—felt it all the way to the bottom of his heart, to the depths of his soul.

Then he turned and walked away.

CHAPTER ELEVEN

OF COURSE it had been longer than half an hour.

Ally knew that. And she knew from the grave look on PJ's face when she'd spotted him in the corridor that he wasn't happy.

But surely he understood she couldn't just leave that very second.

Of course he did, she thought as she hurried outside to find him. And he'd followed her wishes and hadn't come in.

But when she'd come out forty minutes later, he wasn't there.

He hadn't been in the heart center waiting room, and he wasn't in the lobby downstairs. The gift shop—he might have gone to buy a magazine, she thought—was closed. And the cafeteria was empty except for the man mopping the floor.

He'd probably just got tired of waiting and gone out for a walk.

She didn't blame him. She wished she could have brought him in.

But of course it was impossible. Her father was too ill. The slightest upset could cause his condition to deteriorate further. She hadn't needed the nurse to tell her he was fragile.

Nor had she needed the benefit of Jon's medical opinion in the corridor for ten minutes after her dad had fallen asleep again. She knew he was trying to be helpful, to include her. But he was only making her feel guiltier.

She knew she needed to talk to him, to tell him what had

happened. But now was not the time. And she didn't want to hurt Jon, either.

Still, all the time he'd talked, she worried about how to do it, and how to tell her father, and wondered where PJ had got to.

And now that she was outside, she realized that she didn't have a clue where he'd parked the car or even what kind it was. Some late-model metallic silver four door—like hundreds of others—but the model was a mystery.

She looked around, feeling desperate.

"Calm down," she told herself. He'd probably just got tired of waiting and had gone to get something to eat. It had been hours since either of them had eaten. And since the cafeteria wasn't still serving, he'd probably gone to pick them up some sandwiches.

Maybe he'd even gone to Benny's, she thought with a tired smile, then turned and trudged into the hospital again. She'd just go back and sit with her father a while longer. PJ knew where she was, after all.

She wasn't exactly sure how long she sat there before she noticed the suitcase in the corner of her father's room behind the door. It caught her eye because it was tweed and battered and looked exactly like hers.

She eased her hand out of her father's frail grip and went to examine it. Her heart was doing skip-steps in her chest. Her mouth was dry. It couldn't be.

But it was. Her suitcase. Her luggage tag with her address in Honolulu.

She hurried out to the nurse's station. "The bag in my dad's room! Where did it come from?"

"Bag?" The nurse looked confused.

"Suitcase," Ally corrected. "It's mine."

"Oh, yes. The gentleman left it," said another nurse who appeared just then. "You were in with your father and—"

"When?"

"Oh, a couple of hours ago. He said you'd need it."

"Where is he? Where did he go?" Her heart wasn't skip-stepping now. It was flat-out galloping.

Both nurses shrugged. "No idea," one said. "He looked a little ill. Washed out. I asked him if he was all right, if he wanted to sit down. But he just said he had to go."

"Go where?"

Both nurses shrugged. "He went out, came back with the suitcase so you could have it, and then he left."

Just like that.

Left. For good?

Ally felt as if all the breath had been sucked right out of her. As if there wasn't enough air in the whole hospital—in the whole world—to draw in another one.

"Are *you* all right?" one of the nurses demanded.

Ally managed to wet her lips, to stop her knees from shaking. "I'm...fine," she said. "I just...need to go sit down."

And she went back into her father's room. He opened his eyes when the chair squeaked as she sat down.

"My girl," he said in a raspy whisper. His fingers fluttered toward her.

Automatically Ally reached out and put her hand over his. Her father needed her. Her father wanted her. But even as she felt his cool, dry barely responsive fingers in hers, she remembered how the strength of PJ's had supported her all day long.

Until now.

Now he was gone.

It was simple, really, she told herself in the days following PJ's departure as she sat in the hospital and watched her father sleep or stroked his hair or held his hand. PJ didn't love her.

He'd never said he did, after all. He'd taken her to bed, yes. He'd caused her to be limp with longing and hot with desire. He'd made her crazy for him. He'd refused to sign the divorce papers because it was convenient to have a wife.

But he didn't love her.

Did he?

Ten years ago she'd been sure he didn't. The night of their wedding, PJ had made love to her with an eagerness and a gentleness and an awe that still had the power to amaze her, and yet she'd turned her back on it, convinced that it meant nothing.

PJ didn't love her.

Five years ago she'd believed it again. Of course he'd come to her gallery open, eager and smiling and delighted to see her, complimentary and kind, and with a very useful—albeit very beautiful—art critic in tow, but Ally had doubted his intentions, had been suspicious and resentful, sure he was implying that she needed rescuing, that she couldn't do it on her own.

How could he love her when she didn't yet love herself?

And now…?

Now she tried to believe he didn't love her again.

But she couldn't.

Because for the first time nothing in her wanted to believe it. Nothing in her *needed* to believe it. She wasn't afraid of it or of what it would ask of her.

She had the strength and the power and the convictions that came with knowing who she was and that she could be who she wanted to be. It had been a struggle, but it had been worth it.

And she hadn't achieved it alone.

She'd never have got there at all without PJ's gift—and not simply his gift of marrying her ten years ago, but the enduring gift of his love.

PJ Antonides loved her.

He'd walked out of her life, yes, but it wasn't because he didn't love her. It was because he did.

Why would he have brought her all the way back to Hawaii if he didn't care, if he didn't love her?

He could have put her on a plane, washed his hands of her, said so long, farewell, and gone back to his life.

Why would he have taken her out to his parents' house? He hadn't needed her to fend off Connie Cristopolous.

He'd taken her to show her what she was missing. He'd wanted her there because he'd wanted to share his family with her.

Why would he do any of that if he really didn't love her?

It wasn't PJ who didn't love her or who didn't trust love, she realized now.

She was the one. Ally herself.

Or rather, the old Ally. The frightened Ally. The Ally whose mother had died too young and whose father had always seemed to equate love with duty and demands.

But the new Ally—*this* Ally—knew better.

This Ally was beginning to understand now what love was really about. She'd seen it. She'd felt it. She'd held it in her arms.

It was PJ's gift of faith in her ability to become the person she wanted to be. It was his interest and his generosity and his support for who that person was. It was being there—always— but not interfering.

Just believing—in her.

She wasn't exactly sure when she started crying. Didn't mean to. Apologized profusely for frightening the nurses who came running at the sound.

"You're overwhelmed, dear," one of them told her. "You need to get some rest. You should go home for a while. Your father will be all right."

He hadn't heard her sobs. He'd slept right through them. He looked a little better, she thought. More rested. Less fragile.

But what would happen when she told him?

She didn't know.

All her earlier plans were still nice and sensible and eminently doable. She could still get the divorce in due time, marry Jon, have a child, be a mother, make her father happy. She could do it all, just as she'd planned—without PJ.

Because he'd loved her enough to give her that gift.

But if she did, she would do it without the other half of her soul.

* * *

Nobility and self-sacrifice were terrific virtues. They had a lot to recommend them.

But sometimes—like now, PJ thought as he slapped another coat of varnish on the deck of his house, not nearly enough. The sun beat down on his bare back, burning him, and he knew he should put on sunscreen or go inside or put on a shirt.

But the pain of a sunburn might take his mind off Ally.

There was no point in thinking about Ally. The other shoe might have hung around for ten years, but it had finally dropped. He'd signed the divorce papers as soon as he'd got back to New York, and dropped them in the mail.

Yes, he loved her. Yes, he wanted her. And yes, he probably could have convinced her to stay married to him.

But at what cost?

Killing her father?

No. He might be selfish. He might want what he wanted and go after it single-mindedly. But he didn't kill innocent bystanders in the process. Or even not-so-innocent ones.

His back ached. It was a big deck. He wasn't used to this sort of manual labor anymore. "Getting soft," he muttered. It was time to get out from behind that desk.

Elias and Lukas hadn't been thrilled when he'd left.

"How long are you going to be gone?" Lukas had asked.

"Dunno. Need some time."

"Heads of companies don't just up and take off," Elias had said disapprovingly.

"No?" PJ had met his stare with a level one of his own. "Seems I recall you did."

His brothers had muttered and grumbled. "You'll manage," he said flatly. "I'll be back. I need some time."

"Going on your honeymoon?" Lukas had said with a wiggle of his eyebrows.

Elias had kicked him in the shin.

"Hey!" Lukas yelped. "What'd I say?"

"Grow up," Elias growled, "and you'll figure it out."

Was it growing up that did it? PJ wondered. If so, growing up didn't have much to recommend it. It seemed to him he'd been a whole hell of a lot happier before Ally had come back into his life.

But the real hell of it was, he couldn't regret it. Didn't regret it. Still loved her.

And he wasn't sure what the cure was for that.

Jon had been philosophical when she begged off.

"I knew it," he said. "Knew when you went to New York."

"I didn't know it then," Ally argued.

But Jon just smiled a sad knowing smile. "I think you did. I just hope you won't regret it."

So did Ally.

"I wish you the best," he said as they sat across from each other in the hospital cafeteria.

"And I you," she said sincerely. "And I know you will continue to be a good friend to my father."

"Of course," he said. His mouth tipped at one corner. "I am a good doctor."

"And a good friend," Ally insisted. "I'm sure you'll meet someone else. The right person for you, Jon."

Jon smiled politely. "I hope I will."

Ally had no such hope for herself. There was no one else. Just PJ.

So she was gutted when she went home that night to find a priority envelope containing the signed divorce papers in her mailbox.

Ally tried to tell herself that the papers were a part of the gift of his love. And maybe that was true. But they were also a signal that he'd moved on.

How many times could you spurn a man before he said that was enough? Ally knew she didn't want to find out.

She'd have gone back to New York the minute she'd come to her senses if she'd thought her father's health would permit it. But it was one thing to know she wasn't going to marry Jon, and another to tell her father the truth.

But he was out of intensive care now. He was sitting in his private room doing the crossword puzzle these days when she went to see him. He was still frail, but he could walk to the end of the hall.

"Will he die if I tell him we're not getting married?" she'd asked Jon yesterday.

And this time he didn't give her a ten-minute opinion. He simply said, "I hope not."

But he didn't offer to tell her father for her. And she couldn't blame him. The choice not to marry had been hers. So was the obligation to inform her dad.

Just like last time.

This time, though, it was worse, because this time she was afraid that what she was going to say might kill him.

She wanted to wait. But there was no waiting. He'd sensed something was wrong as he'd got better. "You're quiet," he'd said yesterday. "Pale. You have been pale since you got home. You're not well? Ask Jon for something to help you."

She'd shaken her head. "There's nothing Jon can do."

Today he looked up when she came into the room and shook his head in dismay. "No better."

Ally frowned. "You're not?" She thought he looked better.

"Not me. You." He shook his head. "What is wrong, Alice? Are you fighting, you and Jon?"

"No. I—we're not." She wanted to stop there. Knew at the same time she couldn't. "We're not getting married, Dad."

For a long moment her father didn't move. His expression didn't change. He didn't even seem to breathe.

But at least he didn't drop over dead.

"We don't—I don't—" she corrected, knowing she couldn't blame this on Jon "—think it would be a good idea." Pause. She watched her father. *Come on, Dad. Breathe, damn it.* "I don't...I don't love him."

"Love—" Her father got one word out. It seemed to strangle him.

She started to reach for the nurse's bell. He shook his head, held up his hand. Ally waited, coiled with tension.

"Love," he said again. He breathed now, sounding less strangled this time. "Yes. You must have love." His words were raspy, but absolutely clear.

Ally stared at him, then shook her head in disbelief.

"It's true. I know this," he said, nodding slowly, "because of your mother."

"My mother?" Ally's own voice was no more than a croak. Hiroshi Maruyama had never talked about his wife. He'd shut himself away after her mother's death. To Ally it seemed as if the sun had fallen out of the sky. To her father it had just been the excuse for more work.

"I loved your mother," he said slowly. "And sometimes love hurts. When your mother died, I died. Inside. I—didn't want to live without her. So much pain." His eyes seemed to focus on something far off in the distance. They shimmered with unshed tears. And then he looked back at her. "I didn't want you to know such pain, my Alice."

Ally reached out a hand and took his. Thin fingers wrapped hers. Fingers that had some strength to them now. They squeezed. They pressed.

"That is why I wanted you to marry Ken. It was sensible. Not a love match. And if—if something happened—you would not be hurt as I was." He shook his head. "I can be very stupid sometimes."

"No, Dad. You just…cared…"

For me. Ally began to understand that, too. Began to appreciate his motives, if not what he had actually done.

"But I was wrong. I know that now. There is no defense against love. I had your mother for thirteen years. The best thirteen years—" his eyes shone at the memory "—of my life. Not long enough, but worth all the pain. Worth everything. I loved her. For herself. And for you, Alice. For the gift of you."

And then holding his hand wasn't enough. Ally fell to her knees and buried her face in his chest and felt his thin arms come around her, his lips on her hair. Then his arms loosened and he stroked her hair.

She looked up at him, at the tears on his cheeks and closed her eyes when he wiped her own away.

"You love, too," he said. It wasn't a question.

How did he know? She bowed her head and felt his frail fingers stroking her hair and realized that of course he knew. A man who had loved as he had loved would see that love reflected in his daughter's eyes.

She raised her head again and blinked tears from her eyes. "Yes."

"Go to him. Bring him to meet me."

"I'm already married to him, Dad," she said, her voice thick and tremulous.

A faint smile touched his lips. "Good. Then I will have a grandchild soon."

"What do you mean, he's not here?" Ally stared at Rosie, PJ's assistant, feeling as if she'd been punched in the gut.

She'd arrived last night—as soon as she could after her conversation with her father. Coming with his blessing had made her almost sing all the way to New York. She'd gone straight to PJ's apartment, eager to see him. Nervous. Worried.

She'd tried to get hold of him, but she'd never got his cell phone number. And she couldn't call anyone who might have it. She had to see him, to talk to him before anyone else.

And he hadn't been there.

She'd waited until dark. She'd lurked in a nearby café. She'd gone back several times. No PJ.

And now he wasn't here, either?

"When will he be back?"

Rosie shrugged. "No clue."

Not exactly the most professional response. But the way Rosie was looking at her made Ally think she wasn't being given Rosie's best professional demeanor.

"I need to talk to him. Where is he?"

"Don't know that, either," Rosie said. "They might." She jerked her head toward PJ's office door.

"Who?" Ally said. But it didn't matter, really, as long as someone did. She went straight past Rosie and pushed open the slightly ajar door.

Lukas was behind the desk doing something on the computer. Elias was on the floor, and two little boys—his twin sons—were climbing on him while he talked Lukas through some procedure.

They all looked up, startled, when Ally walked in.

Elias recovered first. "About time," he said. "This is all your fault."

Now it was her turn to stare. "What are you talking about?"

"Why I'm here. Why he's—" a thumb in Lukas's direction "—here."

"What? Where's PJ?"

"He's gone. Cut out. Split. Leave of absence."

"Leave of his senses, more like," Lukas muttered.

"Where's he gone? I need to talk to him."

"Talk?" Both his brothers looked at her suspiciously. "About what?"

She hesitated. But she couldn't not say it. She was a believer now. "I love him. I need to tell him."

"Hallelujah," Lukas muttered. "There's hope."

"I hope so," Ally said a little desperately. "Do you know where he is?" It occurred to her that they actually might not.

"Not sure," Elias said, hauling himself up off the floor and making the twins start to cry. He scribbled something on a piece of paper and handed it to her. "Try this. Settle down, guys. I'm coming." And he dropped to the floor again. "Tallie's baking today," he explained. "Some cousin's fancy wedding. So I'm babysitting—and getting Lukas up to speed."

Ally's brows lifted. "To speed."

"Running things," Lukas said grimly. "Hurry up and get him back here. If you don't, I'm going to be stuck being president of Antonides Marine."

Kauai?

She had stared at the address as soon as she got out into the corridor. Why on earth would Elias give her an address in Kauai? She'd just come back from Hawaii. She didn't know anyone in Kauai.

PJ had never mentioned Kauai. It didn't make sense.

But she had to start somewhere, had to take something on faith. So she went.

If she ever found PJ and he told her to get lost, she thought grimly as she battled bloodshot eyes that were gritty from lack of sleep, a rental car with a slipping second gear, and the conviction that she was going on a wild-goose chase, the consolation would have to be all her frequent flyer miles.

She didn't imagine they would make up for the heartbreak, though.

She felt as if she'd been traveling forever. In fact she didn't know what day it was anymore. She'd flown from Honolulu to New York, then back, through San Francisco, to Honolulu and on to Kauai. She hadn't passed Go, she hadn't collected two hundred dollars. She hadn't even stopped to look in on her father.

She didn't want to see the look of disappointment on his face when she turned up without PJ.

And now, it seemed, she was running out of road.

The man at the rental car office had blinked when she'd showed him the address. Then he'd looked it up on his GPS and given her directions. "Out in the boonies," he'd said. "And then some."

He hadn't been lying. The macadam had turned to gravel

a few miles ago, and now the gravel was gone. It had ceased to be any sort of public road and was now not much more than a track.

She knew that there were places in Kauai that were celebrated as "off the beaten path." She just wished she weren't on her way to one of them—especially since she expected to be sent on from there.

She felt like she was going nowhere—just winding through a thick jungly forest, over mountain and down dale. The trees held the heat in. Perspiration trickled down her back. She flexed her shoulders and tried to get rid of the crick in her neck. She wondered if she'd missed a turn. But she hadn't seen anything remotely resembling one.

And then, just as she despaired of ever finding the house, or her way back, she came around a curve and the view opened out into a lush hollow and there was a house—a long stunning Indonesian-style house overhung with palm trees on a rise between her and the sea.

She pulled up as near to the house as she could get. And when the engine shut off, she could hear the sound of birds, the rustle of palm fronds, and waves breaking, and her heart pounding in her chest.

She'd given up even imagining she'd find him. She'd hoped all the way back to New York, all the way to his apartment, all night in her hotel, all the way to his office, all the way back to Kauai, all the way to God knew where.

The house was like something out of Shangri-La—open and airy, with woven shades and soaring lines, all very natural and fitting, built with native stone and wood. The hideout of some wealthy eccentric billionaire no doubt. Certainly not PJ.

Ally grabbed her tote bag out of the car, went up onto the porch and knocked on the door. No one answered. The windows were open, though. Probably the door was, too. Who, after all, would be breaking in out here?

"Anyone home?" she called.

Again no response.

She wasn't driving all the way back again. She simply wasn't. She'd do a Goldilocks and sleep in someone's bed if she had to. Wait for them to come home. Find the next clue...

That was what it felt like.

She tried the door handle. It opened. She hesitated, then just pushed the door open. The inside of the house was as beautiful as the outside, with woven mats on broad-planked teak floors, rattan furniture, a native stone fireplace and eye-catching art—a pair of masks on the wall by the door, a very old surfboard above the sofa. And high on the wall above the fireplace a wall hanging that—

—looked astonishingly familiar.

And yet she hadn't seen it in years.

She stared. Then, numbly she made her way down the shallow steps into the living area to get a closer look.

Believing—and disbelieving—at the same time.

Good heavens, it was here. The one she'd made that first year in California when she'd been so homesick. The one of the beach where she'd met PJ. The ocean in all its shades of blue and green, the houses, shops. The execution was amateurish. She knew that now, had known it then. But it had captured a memory. A time. A place. Things that had meant something special to her but no one else.

And yet someone had bought it. She'd always priced it high—too high for anyone to be tempted. It wasn't that good.

But one day it had been sold.

And now it was here. She reached a hand up and could just reach the bottom of it. She brushed her fingers along the ragged edge of it. And she smiled as she did so.

She didn't need to wonder whose house this was anymore.

She looked around with new eyes. Open eyes. Ran her fingers over the soft patina of the wood. Savored the setting, the way the house and its furnishings fit as if they'd always been there, as if they belonged.

It wasn't a new house. But it had been painstakingly restored. She smelled a bit of varnish, now that she was paying closer attention. She moved to the windows that looked out toward the ocean. Yes, the deck looked as if it had been recently refinished.

And the man who had done it was walking up from the beach.

He was bare-chested, bare-headed, sandy and sunburned. He carried a surfboard under his arm. He looked beautiful. He didn't look happy.

Ally wondered if seeing her would make him any happier.

Or if it was too late. If she'd left it too long.

She took a deep breath and pushed open the door to the deck. It squeaked.

PJ looked up. And stared.

He didn't move. A wave broke against the shore behind him. And then another. He didn't so much as blink. Just stared—and stared—at her.

And then she saw him swallow convulsively. He let out a breath. "Al?" His voice was rusty.

She smiled tentatively, took a step toward him. "You sound worse than the door."

He swallowed again. "Don't…have much occasion to talk." He still didn't move.

She was going to have to make all the running, then. Well, fair enough. She crossed the deck. "Will you talk to me?"

He looked wary. "About what?"

"Coming back to New York." She smiled. "Lukas wants you there."

"I won't go for Lukas."

"Will you come for me?"

There was one more split second of stillness. And then he moved.

He took the three steps that closed the gap between them and wrapped his arms around her, crushed her hard against him, clung to her as if he'd never let her go.

He was shaking, she realized. And so, she thought as her knees wobbled, was she.

"What happened?" he demanded. "Your father...?"

"Wants to meet you."

He stared disbelieving.

She nodded, smiling up at him. "I told him I loved you."

A grin cracked his face. "And he didn't croak?"

She shook her head. "He's sticking around for a grandchild," she told him. "Just like you said."

PJ made a sound somewhere between a laugh and a sob. He wrapped his arms around her again and held her so tightly she nearly couldn't breathe. She didn't care. It felt wonderful. It felt perfect. It felt as if she'd finally come home to the place—and the man—in her life.

Then he eased his grip on her just slightly and drew her into the house with him. "How'd you find me?"

"I went to New York. To your place. You weren't there. I went to the office. Saw Lukas and Elias. I thought Elias was sending me on a wild-goose chase. This is really the...back of the beyond. It's...yours?"

"Bought it five years ago."

"You weren't in New York five years ago," she protested.

"No. But I was tired of hanging around Honolulu. There wasn't much point in staying," he added pointedly.

And there was a look on his face that made her ask wonderingly, "Because of what happened that night—at the gallery?"

"It didn't help."

"No. I'm sorry. I was insecure," she told him. "And there was Annie—" she hated admitting that, but it was true.

"A friend. Period. I swear it."

"I believe you. The problem wasn't you," she told him. "It was me. And now...it's not."

He held her again then, ran his hands over her as if he could barely believe she was here. Then he drew her down onto the sofa and kissed her, and Ally kissed him back, wanting far more than kisses, but needing to get all the explanations out of the way first.

She pulled back to look into his eyes. "I didn't understand," she told him, "about love."

PJ shook his head. "Neither did I. Or maybe I did and it scared me to death. It did that, all right." He let out a breath. "That first night..."

Ally stared at him. "The...first night? Our wedding night?"

"Hell, yeah. You comin' to the door like that. Blew me away. I wasn't ready for it at all."

"It was wonderful," Ally rubbed her thumbs against the backs of his hands.

PJ nodded. "Yeah. But terrifying. Trying to make it good for you—"

"It was good for me," Ally said fervently.

"Well, good. But—not just making love. Making a life...together."

"You...thought about it?"

He let out a breath. "How could I not? But how could I suggest it? I hadn't thought about it before. Wasn't ready to think about it then. And you had things to do. It would have been springing you from one trap to put you in another."

Ally let out a shaky laugh and pushed her hair away from her face as she looked into his. "Oh, God, PJ. I...I wanted it, too. So much. But I couldn't ask for anything more."

They stared at each other a long moment, each of them re-thinking the past, wondering, questioning.

Then PJ said, "Just as well we didn't. We'd probably have blown it."

And Ally bit her lip and nodded, certain he was right. But she had to ask, "What about when I came back to Honolulu five years ago? Were you ready then?"

"I thought I might be." He shoved a hand through his hair, then added wryly, "Not that I had anything to offer you then."

"You'd already given me everything I could ever have

wanted." She framed his face in her hands and kissed him again. It was a long kiss, a lingering kiss. A kiss that allowed her to realize, dear God, how much she loved him—and how long.

"I love you," she murmured. "So much. I think I always did. But I didn't know how to tell you. Or to trust it."

"And now you do?" It was a statement, but Ally heard the question in it.

"I do," Ally said, and smiled at the echo of her vow so many years ago. "See?" And she turned her side to him so that he could see a small fabric patch she'd appliqued to her sleeve.

PJ studied the pair of entwined fabric hearts. His mouth twitched. "You're wearing your heart on your sleeve."

"I am," she agreed. "Always. For you. I just didn't know how to tell you."

"Just say the words," he told her hoarsely. "You can't ever say them enough."

So Ally said them again. And again. She put her arms around his neck as he swung her up and cradled her against him as he carried her inside. "I love you, PJ Antonides. I will tell you so every day of your life."

"Works for me," he said. "You can show me, too." He grinned, carrying her all the way into the bedroom. "Anytime you want."

She showed him how much she loved him while they stayed on Kauai. She showed him back in Honolulu when they stayed a week to visit with her dad.

Far from having died at the news of who she was in love with, Hiroshi Maruyama seemed to have a new lease on life. Certainly he did his best to make PJ feel welcome. And so what if he dropped more than a few hints about how nice it would be to have a grandchild.

"I'm willing," PJ said. "Whenever Ally is."

"We're working on it," she assured her father, blushing when he smiled knowingly.

She was gratified that PJ and her father got on well. But

she was equally happy when PJ said he needed to get back to New York.

"Wouldn't want Lukas to think I'd abandoned him forever."

"I'm looking forward to getting home," Ally replied.

PJ's brows lifted. "Home." He grinned. "I like it that you're coming home with me."

"I liked—I love—everything about you," Ally assured him. "And I want to get back to look at the mural."

And now they were home in PJ's Park Slope brownstone— her home, Ally thought with abiding joy. And she was standing in front of the mural, looking. And looking. And looking.

"I'm not here," she said.

She looked at everyone in the beach scenes. She didn't find anyone who looked like her. She identified many of the others—surfers they knew, friends they'd had, even her own friend May. But she couldn't find herself.

Or PJ for that matter. He wasn't on the beach. He wasn't in the water. He wasn't anywhere.

She studied Benny's Place. Maybe he was eating a hamburger there. Maybe she was behind the counter. But neither was there. She looked at the anonymous passersby just ambling by on the sidewalks or sunning on the shore.

"We're not here," she grumbled.

PJ came and stood behind her, wrapping his arms around her, nuzzling beneath her ear. "You're looking in the wrong place."

"I've looked every place we were. The beach. The sand. Benny's." Ally sighed.

"You'll find it. You've got the rest of our lives."

She smiled and settled back against him, loving the feel of his hard strong arms holding her. She turned her head and planted a kiss on his jaw, then went back to the mural. She found the university, the surf shop where PJ had worked, the tiny hole-in-the-wall storage unit where he had built his first windsurfers. She found the apartment where he'd lived above Mrs. Chang's garage.

"Ah." She tapped at the tiny painted window. "Are we in there?"

PJ nipped her ear and laughed. "It's not an X-rated mural."

But she was beginning to feel a bit X-rated right now. His hands were sliding up under her shirt, cupping her breasts. She could feel PJ's body, behind hers, developing its own X-rated agenda.

And then, just when she was about to give up and suggest they adjourn to the bedroom, she found them—PJ and Ally—kissing on the steps of the courthouse.

Ally stared in amazement. She felt shivers all up and down her spine because it was such a pivotal memory for her. And that he would have chosen it, too...

"That's your memory of us? Not the beach? Not Benny's? You remember kissing at the courthouse?"

"What's wrong with the courthouse?" PJ wanted to know.

"Nothing's wrong. It's just—I can't believe that's what you remember." It was like a gift. The greatest gift—his love.

"It's not all I remember. But it's what I remember most," he said as he turned her in his arms and kissed her again—and again and again and again. Then he drew her with him down the hall and into the bedroom.

"It was the start of what I want to remember always, Al." And as they fell together onto their bed, he wrapped his arms around her and kissed her with all the urgency they'd both felt that day. "It's when I first began to believe in love."

Demure but defiant...
Can three international playboys
tame their disobedient brides?

Lynne Graham

presents

Proud, masculine and passionate, these men are used
to having it all. In stories filled with drama, desire
and secrets of the past, find out how these arrogant
husbands capture their hearts.

THE GREEK TYCOON'S DISOBEDIENT BRIDE
Available December 2008, Book #2779

THE RUTHLESS MAGNATE'S VIRGIN MISTRESS
Available January 2009, Book #2787

THE SPANISH BILLIONAIRE'S PREGNANT WIFE
Available February 2009, Book #2795

EXTRA

HIRED: FOR THE BOSS'S PLEASURE

She's gone from personal assistant
to mistress—but now he's demanding
she become the boss's bride!

Read all our fabulous stories this month:

MISTRESS: HIRED FOR THE BILLIONAIRE'S PLEASURE
by INDIA GREY

THE BILLIONAIRE BOSS'S INNOCENT BRIDE
by LINDSAY ARMSTRONG

HER RUTHLESS ITALIAN BOSS
by CHRISTINA HOLLIS

MEDITERRANEAN BOSS, CONVENIENT MISTRESS
by KATHRYN ROSS

HPE0209

HARLEQUIN *Presents*

International Billionaires

*Life is a game of power and pleasure.
And these men play to win!*

Let Harlequin Presents® take you on a jet-set journey
to meet eight male wonders of the world. From rich
tycoons to royal playboys— they're red-hot and ruthless!

International Billionaires coming in 2009

THE PRINCE'S WAITRESS WIFE
by *Sarah Morgan,* February

AT THE ARGENTINEAN BILLIONAIRE'S BIDDING
by *India Grey,* March

THE FRENCH TYCOON'S PREGNANT MISTRESS
by *Abby Green,* April

THE RUTHLESS BILLIONAIRE'S VIRGIN
by *Susan Stephens,* May

THE ITALIAN COUNT'S DEFIANT BRIDE
by *Catherine George,* June

THE SHEIKH'S LOVE-CHILD
by *Kate Hewitt,* July

BLACKMAILED INTO THE GREEK TYCOON'S BED
by *Carol Marinelli,* August

THE VIRGIN SECRETARY'S IMPOSSIBLE BOSS
by *Carol Mortimer,* September

8 volumes in all to collect!

REQUEST YOUR FREE BOOKS!

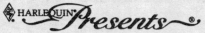 

2 FREE NOVELS
PLUS 2
FREE GIFTS!

YES! Please send me 2 FREE Harlequin Presents® novels and my 2 FREE gifts (gifts are worth about $10). After receiving them, if I don't wish to receive any more books, I can return the shipping statement marked "cancel". If I don't cancel, I will receive 6 brand-new novels every month and be billed just $4.05 per book in the U.S. or $4.74 per book in Canada, plus 25¢ shipping and handling per book and applicable taxes, if any*. That's a savings of close to 15% off the cover price! I understand that accepting the 2 free books and gifts places me under no obligation to buy anything. I can always return a shipment and cancel at any time. Even if I never buy another book, the two free books and gifts are mine to keep forever.

106 HDN ERRW 306 HDN ERRL

Name	(PLEASE PRINT)	
Address		Apt. #
City	State/Prov.	Zip/Postal Code

Signature (if under 18, a parent or guardian must sign)

Mail to the Harlequin Reader Service:
IN U.S.A.: P.O. Box 1867, Buffalo, NY 14240-1867
IN CANADA: P.O. Box 609, Fort Erie, Ontario L2A 5X3

Not valid to current subscribers of Harlequin Presents books.

Want to try two free books from another line?
Call 1-800-873-8635 or visit www.morefreebooks.com.

* Terms and prices subject to change without notice. N.Y. residents add applicable sales tax. Canadian residents will be charged applicable provincial taxes and GST. Offer not valid in Quebec. This offer is limited to one order per household. All orders subject to approval. Credit or debit balances in a customer's account(s) may be offset by any other outstanding balance owed by or to the customer. Please allow 4 to 6 weeks for delivery. Offer available while quantities last.

Your Privacy: Harlequin Books is committed to protecting your privacy. Our Privacy Policy is available online at www.eHarlequin.com or upon request from the Reader Service. From time to time we make our lists of customers available to reputable third parties who may have a product or service of interest to you. If you would prefer we not share your name and address, please check here. ☐

HP08R

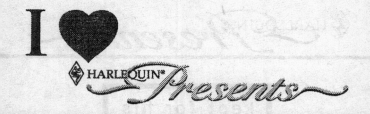

kept for his
Pleasure

She's his mistress on demand!

Wherever seduction takes place, these fabulously
wealthy, charismatic, sexy men know how to
keep a woman coming back for more!

She's his mistress on demand—but when he
wants her body *and soul* he will be demanding
a whole lot more! Dare we say it…even marriage!

CONFESSIONS OF A
MILLIONAIRE'S MISTRESS
by *Robyn Grady*

Don't miss any books in
this exciting new miniseries
from Harlequin Presents!